William Salter

Memoirs of Joseph W. Pickett
missionary superintendent in southern Iowa and in the Rocky mountains for the American home missionary society

ISBN/EAN: 9783337287580

Printed in Europe, USA, Canada, Australia, Japan

Cover: Foto ©Raphael Reischuk / pixelio.de

More available books at **www.hansebooks.com**

MEMOIRS

OF

JOSEPH W. PICKETT,

*Missionary Superintendent in Southern Iowa and in the Rocky
Mountains for the American Home Missionary Society.*

By WILLIAM SALTER.

So close is glory to our dust,
So near is God to man,
When Duty whispers low, Thou must,
The youth replies, I can.
—*Emerson.*

BURLINGTON, IOWA: JAMES LOVE.
COLORADO SPRINGS, COLORADO: MRS. S. B. PICKETT.
1880.

For sale by the Congregational Publishing Society, Boston, Mass.

CONTENTS.

CHAPTER I.

EARLY LIFE, ANCESTRY, EDUCATION.

CHAPTER II.

MINISTRY AT WENTWORTH, N.H., AND MOUNT PLEASANT, IOWA.

CHAPTER III.

SUPERINTENDENT OF HOME MISSIONS IN SOUTHERN IOWA.

CHAPTER IV.

SUPERINTENDENT AND GENERAL MISSIONARY IN THE ROCKY MOUN-
TAINS.

Contents.

MEMOIRS

OF

JOSEPH W. PICKETT.

CHAPTER I.

EARLY LIFE, ANCESTRY, EDUCATION.

JOSEPH WORTHY PICKETT was born at Andover, Ashtabula County, Ohio, January 28, 1832. His ancestors were among the early settlers of New England, who left the mother country in the Puritan emigration of the reign of Charles I. He was of the sixth generation from John Pickett, who came from the County of Kent, England; settled in Salem, Conn., 1648; moved to Stratford, 1660, and died April 11, 1684. The following is the line of descent:—

1. Daniel, 1652–1688.

2. Samuel, 1682–1761.

3. John, 1716 — February, 1807; married Elizabeth Meeker; moved to Sandisfield, Berkshire County, Mass.

4. John, June, 1753 — October, 1840; married Ruth Boardman, 1759 — March 25, 1806, of Middletown, Conn. He was a soldier of the Revolution; representative from Sandisfield in the Massachusetts Con-

vention of 1788, which ratified the Constitution of the
United States ; and in the House of Representatives of
Massachusetts from 1789 to 1796, and from 1804 to
1813 ; also a justice of peace for many years in the
same town ; and moved to the unbroken forest of
North-eastern Ohio in 1819, with his three sons, John,
Joseph, and

5. Benjamin, July 22, 1795 — April 26, 1873 ; married
Lydia Ophelia Birchard, of Crawford County, Penn.,
January 8, 1822.

6. Joseph W.

His mother is a native of Becket, Berkshire County,
Mass., and of the sixth generation from Thomas Birchard, who was born at Roxbury, England, in 1595 ;
came from England in the ship "True Love," 1635 ;
was made a freeman of Boston, 1637 ; settled at Say-
brook, Conn., and died 1684.   This is her line of
descent : —

1. John, one of the original proprietors of Norwich,
Conn.

2. James, 1665–1745.

3. James, 1699–1786 ; moved, 1755, to Becket.

4. James, 1731–1820 ; one of the first selectmen, and
the first treasurer of Becket. His only son was

5. James.

In the autumn of 1812, he started with his family, the
oldest child eighteen, the youngest two years of age,
for the "Far West."   They carried their household
goods, provisions, and bedding in one heavy wagon,
drawn by two yoke of oxen and a horse.   Another

wagon, drawn by three horses, took lighter articles and the family. Many were the mishaps and hardships of the wilderness. Now and then the wagons were upset or stuck in the mud. Several nights were spent with no shelter but the woods. For one hundred and fifty miles, they passed down the Alleghany River in flat-boats. After six weeks' weary travel, they reached the tract that had been selected for their home, seven miles north of Meadville, Penn. Here, coming some years afterward as a teacher into an adjoining school district, Benjamin Pickett found his wife.

6. Lydia, born November 29, 1802.

Andover was then a township in the woods, five miles square. No roads had been made on its eastern side, where Benjamin Pickett had located. The only guides in going from place to place were blazed trees. The new home was a log structure, without window or chimney, the apertures between the unchinked logs furnishing light, and an opening in the roof carrying off the smoke. Thus they lived for the first year. Most of the neighbors were newly married people, and similarly situated. As busy years rolled on, the land was cleared for pasture and tillage, additions and improvements were made to the cabin, and support and comfort secured for the growing family. Here the subject of this memoir was born, the fifth of eight children.

He early showed conscientiousness, truthfulness, and a love of knowledge. Before he was three years old, he would place two chairs facing each other, and coax

his elder brother to read to him. At .five, he was a
good reader. Warm in filial feeling, he loved to help
his mother on washing days, gathering wood for her
fire by the brook, and sharing her simple lunch in the
shade. As he grew in strength, he assisted his father
in the heavy labors of the farm. These were the happy
memories of his childhood.

When seven years old, his father gave him a pocket-
knife, greatly to his delight. The need of a new house
was at that time the household talk. The children's
hearts were set upon it. But the careful father, scan-
ning the cost and his resources in the presence of the
family, decided that he could not afford to build. This
filled Joseph with sorrow. With tears in his eyes, he
went into the forest to weep and think by himself. As
he reflected that his father could not build for want of
means, he remembered that his new knife had cost
something, and he at once resolved what to do. He
returned to the cabin, handed the treasure to his father,
and said: "Here is my knife, father. Take it back to
the store, and get the money. I can do without it."
The father's heart was touched to tears, and he said,
"Joseph, keep your knife, and we will build the new
house." The willing self-sacrifice of the boy had
kindled new energy in the man. There was no more
faltering until the family moved into a new house, one
of the best appointed dwellings in the township. It
stands upon a hill, close to a charming piece of woods
of fifty acres. Hon. Ben. Wade, visiting here when
the orchard was in full bloom, called it one of the
pleasantest places he ever saw.

The charm and beauty of nature won the boy's heart. He remembered through life the impressions which flowers and woods and the south wind made upon him when five years of age. In after years, Ruskin was one of his favorite authors.

He attended school a portion of each year in a log school-house three-quarters of a mile distant, until he was sixteen, when he entered the academy in Kingsville, on the shore of Lake Erie, for the fall term. At nineteen, he entered Alleghany College, at Meadville, Penn. Obliged to practise close economy, he rented a room, obtained provisions from home, did his own cooking, and frequently managed to live upon fifty cents a week. In the Junior year, he took the Haseltine Prize Medal for the best English composition. He graduated in 1855. His theme at Commencement was "Plato and his Philosophy." While in the academy and at college, he taught school during the winter months. Showing a superior faculty for instruction, he won the hearts of scholars, and gained honor and esteem in every community where he was employed. He thus obtained means to defray the expenses of his own education.

From early youth, he took part in literary and debating societies, and won repute as a ready speaker and an ingenious and able disputant. In the political canvass of 1848, he listened to the humor and eloquence of Thomas Corwin and to the strong and persuasive arguments of Joshua R. Giddings.

The heavy work upon the farm was haying. At that

2

season, Joseph always arranged to be at home, and, with his scythe and rake and pitchfork, and cheering laugh and persistent pluck, made "the best of hands," as his father called him.

He cherished through life the memory of an interest in religion when eight years of age. His father gathered the children around the family altar. His mother's devotional nature gave him a constant nurture of grace and goodness. At eighteen, when a student at Kingsville Academy, a brother's sudden death deepened his serious convictions. During his first year in college, in a time of awakening, he sought the Lord through weeks of fasting and prayer, with strong crying and tears. The hills of Meadville were witness to his spiritual struggles. When it pleased God to reveal his Son in him, and he saw the divine love in Jesus Christ, he acted with prompt decision, and on the following Saturday walked home, twenty-four miles, to unite with the church of his fathers at the communion on the next day. An extract from his diary of this period shows his fervor and devotion : —

After the five o'clock prayer-meeting this morning, Merrill and I proceeded to the forests, where for two hours we supplicated at the throne of grace, and received largely of the Holy Spirit. I was enabled through faith to behold Christ's kingdom, and saw the ancient prophets worshipping around the throne. Oh, the holy joy of believing! I desire to give up my body as the temple of the Holy Spirit. May God ever guide me in the strait and narrow path!

Many years later, he said of his habits of retirement for meditation and prayer : —

I used to walk miles every day, going to some quiet retreat,

where I walked backward and forward, talking aloud to God, sometimes repeating portions of Scripture. I have worn paths in the deep woods so hard that the grass would not grow for months. Then I would kneel in prayer. I shall never forget those seasons. They sweetened my life, took out selfishness and passion, and put in sweetness and love, and a longing desire to do others good.

Before leaving college, he had made an engagement to take charge of an academy at Taylorsville, Wilson County, Tenn., but after reaching home was prostrated with typhoid fever, and brought very low. Upon convalescence, he was urged to delay. But, feeling that strength would come as he went on his way, he left home the last of August. It was his first long journey, and his first travel by railroad. His health improved every day. From Louisville, he went by stage to his destination, thirty-seven miles east of Nashville. Here was his work for two years. The academy flourished in his hands. He aroused a generous ambition among the students, and imparted to them his moral vigor and spiritual force. A neighboring hill of shady oaks and moss-covered rocks was his chosen resort for exercise and for meditation and prayer.

In the summer vacation of 1856, he travelled into East Tennessee and North Carolina, alone, on horseback; making observations of the geology of those regions, and enjoying the wildness and grandeur of the scenery. He visited Bon Air Springs, Roane County, and passed up Clinch River to Knoxville. From the Cumberland Mountains, he wrote, August 2d :—

I stayed Wednesday night at a tavern kept by an Ohio man. I told him it was the last thing I expected,— to see a man leaving

Ohio for these barren mountains. He came for his health, he said. There are good reasons for its being healthy upon the mountains : a person can seldom get enough to eat to make him sick. I felt sorry for the landlady. She could get along, she said, if they had any privileges ; that there was no school, and only now and then preaching, Baptist and Methodist, but neither of the preachers could read. Of course, there are exceptions to this gloomy aspect of the region. Now and then I call upon a wealthy, intelligent farmer who is a perfect gentleman. The political fever runs high. It will be a tight match between Fillmore and Buchanan. I know little of Northern politics.

From Knoxville, he went to Dandridge, and up French Broad River to the Warm Springs, N.C., six miles from the State line, a fashionable resort for the sons and daughters of fortune from the South. Riding on through Buncombe County, he ascended Mount Mitchell August 14th, and from its top wrote : —

My *highest* desire is realized and my *loftiest* aspiration gratified, for I stand upon the far-famed mount, the loftiest summit of the Blue Ridge and highest point east of the Rocky Mountains. Having put on a thick overcoat which belongs to one of the men who are clearing the top of the mountain, I have ascended the rude observatory made of balsam-trees, and am gazing upon the scene. Nothing I have before witnessed will bear comparison with it. But it is cold. I must go to a fire the workmen have built under a ledge of rock. . . . This is comfortable ; and I must tell you of my adventures. Yesterday, it rained most of the forenoon ; dark clouds hung around the mountains. At dinner, I saw some speckled trout the boys had caught. I remembered the stories father had told me, and determined to go fishing. The boys got bait. We went up the mountain about two miles by the side of a dashing, foaming stream, passing high laurel and ivy bushes that were growing in luxuriance, and threw in our hooks. I watched the boy's motion until I saw the plan, and then com-

menced. I let my hook float along the stream, when up came a trout and snapped it. I drew him out. Leaping along the rocks, I let my hook dance into the deep holes, when up came another fellow, which I ousted. It was the greatest sport at fishing I ever had. I caught five, the boy three. He said it was the first time he was ever beaten.

This morning, about seven, with a son of my host, I started up the mountain on foot. We travelled on and on. I made him puff and blow. We reached here between one and two o'clock this afternoon, after ten miles of "up-hill business." My host and several hands are at work here, building a sleeping-room. I am going to see the sun and moon rise and set. I can stand it to stay under the rocks without cover, if these mountaineers can. So good-night.

Morning, August 15.— I slept most of the night finely. We had a large fire built, which we were obliged to replenish often, as the fir-wood is poor to keep fire. My thermometer stood at 45° this morning. The sun set behind a cloud last night, but its rising this morning was glorious. The fog resembles vast lakes, above which the mountain summits rear their heads like islands.

His return to Middle Tennessee was by another route, through Jackson, Macon, and Cherokee Counties, N.C., and Monroe County, Tenn. Passing over the ancient domain of the Cherokee Indians, he entered a lonely valley, some thirty miles wide, with the ragged and rocky crags of the Blue Ridge on one side and the Smoky Mountains on the other. Overwhelmed at times by the towering, precipitous grandeur of the former, he found a fascination and charm in the soft and restful splendor of the latter. It was long an image in his mind of "the valley of blessing." On one side towered the holy law; on the other, the divine love seemed diffused abroad.

On the fifteenth of September, he resumed his work at the academy, with an increased number of pupils and his brother Cyrus as assistant. He closed his labors there July 10, 1857, with grateful assurances of esteem from his pupils, and with promises of a prayerful remembrance of them on his part. Five of his pupils accompanied him home, to be educated at Alleghany College. Three remained North, and a few years later joined the army of the Union. One was first lieutenant of a college company raised at Meadville; assistant adjutant-general at the battle of Dranesville, December 20, 1861 ; fought bravely on the Peninsula and before Richmond, and died from exhaustion. The others raised a company of cavalry, of which one was captain and the other first lieutenant.

Having saved twelve hundred and fifty dollars from his earnings in teaching, Mr. Pickett was enabled to pursue a cherished plan of study at Yale College, where he joined the Senior class, and graduated in 1858. He greatly prized the opportunities for culture afforded him at New Haven. Though not in firm health, he pursued his studies vigorously, and made more broad and solid his foundations for usefulness. His heart was deeply enlisted in the revival of religion which that year blessed the college. In Professor Goodrich, he recognized a model man.

In the fall of 1858, he entered the Theological Seminary at Andover, Mass., and pursued the full course of study for three years with industry and zeal. Not neglecting opportunities of usefulness or the culture of the

heart, he labored frequently in religious meetings and Bible classes, and, amid the walks and woods of Andover, kept up his habits of communion with nature and of devout meditation. During his first winter there, he wrote : —

Our oceanic winds and rain-storms are a conglomeration of hail, sleet, and snow, which loads the trees ; but, let it come pleasant when they are thus adorned, and it is difficult to conceive of anything more beautiful. A week since, a damp, frosty snow fell upon the trees during the night and arranged itself in crystals, so that the morning revealed as glorious a spectacle as one could imagine. As we passed between the elms that interweave their branches above our walks, covered with millions of crystals, I remarked to my classmate that never did royal monarch walk beneath a more gorgeous canopy.

During the summer vacation of 1859, he labored under the Vermont Home Missionary Society at North Hyde Park and Eden, Lamoille County, but overtaxed himself, and was laid aside by sickness. He recovered so as to return to the seminary, but was again prostrated for several weeks. Upon regaining his health, such was his ardor and devotion that he soon made up all he had lost in his prescribed studies.

CHAPTER II.

MINISTRY AT WENTWORTH, N.H., AND MOUNT PLEASANT, IOWA.

TOWARD the close of his seminary course, he was invited to return to North Hyde Park, being "the one that always came to mind as the minister they needed." But his steps were directed to Wentworth, Grafton County, N.H., where he found a happy field of labor for two years, among an intelligent and a refined people, who appreciated the devotion and kindling fervor of his ministry, and invited him to become their pastor. A work of grace prevailed during much of the time. Eighteen were added to the church by profession, and twelve by letter. He was ordained an Evangelist at Bristol, N.H., January 2, 1862, in company with a classmate, Rev. C. F. Abbott. The sermon was preached by Cyrus W. Wallace, D.D., and the ordaining prayer offered by Rev. Liba Conant. A few months afterward, April 10, he was united in marriage at West Williamsfield, Ohio, with Miss Mary Jane, daughter of Rev. George and Ann J. (Marvin) Roberts, a lady of gentle ways and sunny disposition, inheriting the faith and devotion of her lamented father, whose praise is in the churches of North-eastern Ohio to this day. He died May 7, 1857.

At Wentworth, Mr. Pickett's enjoyment of nature

was intense. The strength of the hills was his delight.
A short distance from his home is a lofty hill, covered
with evergreens and maples, and affording a fine prospect. Thither he resorted almost daily, book in hand,
to read and study and pray. There he poured out his
heart for the country,— it was at the commencement of
the Rebellion,— and revolved the questions of going to
the war as a private soldier or chaplain, of entering
the foreign missionary field, or going to the Far West,
or remaining in New England. The hill was soon
called " Pickett's Hill," and still retains the name. He
visited it whenever in after years he went to Wentworth.   In 1861 and in 1862, he made a tour to the
White Mountains, and again, at a later day, with his
two boys.

To leave this delightful region and his pleasant associations with the Church cost him no little struggle.
But a voice seemed to say: " Other fields have been
appointed you. Up, and away to your life-work!" The
claims of Portland, Oregon, and of fields in Nebraska
and Missouri, and the wants of Iowa, were pressed
upon his attention. On leaving, the Church expressed
their appreciation of him as "a diligent and faithful
laborer, spiritually-minded, abounding in prayers, and
a ready and able speaker, rightly divining the Word."
He had found the Church weak : he left it strong. His
heart often reverted to this field. " We long for the
hills," he wrote. " I want the mayflowers every spring,
and a leaf from the old maple-tree that shaded my
window, and something from ' Pickett's Hill ' every

autumn." After removing to Colorado, he wrote:
"Our home faces Pike's Peak and glorious mountain
scenery. But its vast and varied grandeur is not yet
so precious to me as the sweet beauty of New Hamp-
shire's hills, and her rushing watercourses."

During the summer of 1863, he visited the West to
see its condition and wants, and look at fields that were
calling for laborers. He spent several weeks at Council Bluffs and Nebraska City, and was urged by a little
band of struggling Christians in each place to remain
with them. In Nebraska City, he preached a vigorous
discourse on the day of National Thanksgiving for the
victories at Vicksburg and Gettysburg, that was cheering to the friends of the country in that community,
where a powerful secession element had existed from
the beginning of the war.

On the 12th of August, he visited Mount Pleasant,
Henry County, Iowa. The opportunity of usefulness
there, with the cordial welcome given him, seemed a
divine call to that field. Here he spent the next six
years, laboring with fervor and diligence, carrying the
gospel into destitute neighborhoods, helping the schools,
promoting the cause of temperance, addressing public
meetings in each township in the county for the Bible
Society, of which he was president, enlisting in every
effort for the improvement of society, and raising the
church from dependence upon the Missionary Society
to self-support.

Of free and cordial manners, he won men to him.
He had remarkable facility and despatch in visiting

from house to house, and had a word in season for every person, from the oldest to the youngest. No one was too humble for his care. In highways and by-ways, he sought out the wandering. His genial spirit, his untiring and ·ungrudging labors, made for him a host of friends outside his congregation. In his favorite work of evangelism among outlying districts, he was swift of foot, often performing feats of pedestrianism ; walking long distances to preaching stations, and allowing neither extreme heat nor severe cold nor muddy roads nor storms nor swollen streams to detain him from appointments. On one occasion, in winter, finding the ice gone on which he expected to cross a creek, he stripped off his lower clothing, and "waded in." He got safely over, dressed himself, went on his way, and fulfilled his appointment. He had preached that morning in Mount Pleasant. He returned there on a hand-car, working his passage part of the way, and preached again at night. He organized churches at Rome and Hickory Grove,—one eight miles west, and the other five miles north, of Mount Pleasant. Reviewing his work with the latter Church, at the dedication of their house of worship, in 1870, he wrote : —

As I looked upon the beautiful church, crowded with people, my heart was filled with gratitude at the thought of what God has wrought. Less than three years since, the church was organized with fear and trembling in a small, wretched, old school-house, where I had preached for some months, without even a desk to lay my Bible on. Now a membership of fifty earnest Christians gathered from all classes is making its influence felt through the region. It procured aid from the Congregational Union to the

amount of two hundred dollars, but has not asked a cent from the Home Missionary Society, and is free from debt.

In July and August, 1864, he visited the scenes of the war in Tennessee and Georgia, at the call of the Christian Commission, to carry the ministry of religion among the sick and wounded soldiers. The following extracts are from his letters while in that service :—

July 12, 1864. — At Louisville, everything is changed from what it was seven years ago. Military officers now occupy the place of the Southern chivalry. Troops were marching here and there through the city, some hurrying to the front, others returning. Thursday we started for Nashville. Soldiers with muskets and bayonets stood at the doors of the cars. Nine years ago, I had gone in a stage over this route. War has changed the appearance of the country ; but few crops are being raised, and these very poor. At Munfordsville, I saw the first rebel works. Long lines of rifle-pits had been constructed, and other fortifications, all now deserted. Here a vast rebel army flushed with hope once confronted us. Onward to the South, mile upon mile, we moved, past rebel works which are now in our hands. I never realized before how much we have done toward putting down the Rebellion. We came in sight of the Cumberland River, on whose banks I once spent so many happy days ; but now everything speaks of desolation. Bristling bayonets guard the whole way. We found Nashville full to overflowing of military men. The Christian Commission occupy a large house in the city, owned by a rebel, who had run away with his family. He left the most of his furniture, which was convenient for us. On the second floor, in the hall was a nice baby-carriage. The nest was there, but the birdie had flown. I hope the little one will not be nursed into a rebel.

In the morning, I rose at daylight, found it raining ; and in the rain, far up and down the street, was a cavalry regiment. I walked out to see them, and asked, " What regiment is this ? " " Fifth Iowa Cavalry," said they. " Where are you bound ? "

"We do not know." They had started from camp at midnight, to leave at two o'clock in the morning; but for some reason did not go. I was glad to find a regiment from our State, and went around among them.

After breakfast, we filled our haversacks with books, papers, and writing material, and started for Cumberland Hospital, about one mile out of the city. Here are several hundred large tents, with over three thousand sick and wounded in rows of low beds. Coming to one of the tents, I would say, as cheerfully as I could, "Good-morning, soldiers! How do you all do?" They would turn their pale, ghastly faces with a questioning look. "I have come to cheer you," said I. "Have brought you books and papers from home. The loved ones think of you, and pray for you." Then you ought to have seen the smile and the welcome, as from tent to tent I distributed my papers, and told the dear boys of home. I found all kinds of wounds. Many were wounded in the head; some, in the eye; some, in the back, so that they had to lie on their faces; some with legs off; some with arms off. I ask, "Where were you wounded?" Many reply, "At Kenesaw Mountain." Nearly half of the present wounded are from that gory field. I am tired of the very name. I entered one tent, and said, "You do not get discouraged, do you?" "Oh, no!" said one: "we do not allow any blues here. It will do no good." I looked at him. There he lay, with his leg amputated above the knee! I thought, "That is courage, which would do well for faint hearts at home."

We left Nashville on a hospital train, full of beds which lay on boards adapted to the purpose. It looked like work to see a long train of cars pushing to the front, to be filled with wounded and dying men. At every little bridge was a stockade, where we threw out papers to men eager to read. At Tullahoma, I held two services on the Sabbath in the wards of the hospital. Some were so sick I did not dare to be long.

We found the road full of wild interest,—watched for bush-whackers, saw three or four places where trains had been thrown off a few days before by torpedoes. At one place, the cars ran into one another two weeks ago, the passenger train full of

wounded men. A large number were killed, and others worse wounded.

At Stevenson, Ala., we went to the Soldiers' Home, formerly "Alabama House," where Jeff. Davis made his speech. I never realized the blessings of home so much as when we went to our miserable bed. In the morning, we visited a colored school. The children and grown girls and boys sat on low, narrow seats, in a leaky house, without a floor, with bare feet and dresses draggling in water and mud. The teacher was from Wisconsin, and seemed discouraged. She said that the people were abused. We heard a class read that showed remarkable aptitude.

Here we fell in with a quartermaster who proved to be an old acquaintance, Captain Warren, of Jackson County, who procured horses for us; and we rode far out beyond the pickets, but saw nothing to frighten us, only dead horses and mules. Alone, I ascended a mountain, two miles to the summit, where I got a splendid view of the village, with its fortifications and surrounding mountains.

Chattanooga, Tenn., July 15.—From Stevenson to this point, the country is mountainous; stockades, only a short distance apart, over the whole route. We passed beneath the frowning cliffs which, rising perpendicular from the river, mark the first bench of Lookout Mountain. The town is full of fortifications, soldiers, black and white; while Lookout Mountain looms above us, full of native as well as historic grandeur. Mission Ridge, in full view, stretches about two miles away to the south of us, while the broad Tennessee hugs the northern side.

I am sad and sick at heart. It seems almost wrong to look toward my own sweet home and think how soon I am to enjoy it, when so many are suffering and in agony, with no hope of seeing loved ones again. I do not know whether it is best to tell you of all I have seen and heard to-day; yet perhaps you can endure a few words as well as I could the whole day. But what is this to all the poor soldiers suffer? I was assigned to Hospital No. 1, where are the worst cases of wounds. Men who were brought

from the battle on cars, and could not be moved farther, were left at this, the nearest hospital. Nearly all the wounded had legs off above the knee. They lay in the oppressive heat, with a bandage on the limb, fanning, to keep the swarms of flies off. Here, a nurse was washing a limb which looked like raw, spoiled meat. In one tent, a young man's face was literally black with flies. They had crawled between his lips. I took a fan and brushed them away, and talked with him. I asked him where he was from. How strange it sounded! "Ashtabula County, Ohio; from Dorset." Was attending Kingsville Academy when he enlisted. He said, "I wish I was back again." And well he might, for he would probably live but a few days.

In one of the long buildings I entered, there lay a poor fellow struggling in awful agony. His amputated limb had become so bad that they reamputated it a few hours before, and now he was dying. Opposite, the nurse was dressing the leg of a noble-looking fellow whose limb had been amputated near the hip, picking off decayed matter with a pair of forceps. It was a terrible sight. He groaned each time they touched it, and pleaded with them not to be so harsh. The flesh had decayed over the end of the limb, and been removed, leaving great holes. After they were through, "Hand me the glass," he said; and, reaching down, held it so as to reflect the end of the limb, and asked: "Doctor, you said it looked better. Are those deep, black holes better? I cannot see it." Poor fellow! The doctor says the chances are against him. On farther was a man nearly gone, who mingled with others' groans the singing of Psalms. I passed on to some quiet sufferers, and said, "Is not this a hard place for you?" "Oh, yes," they said. "It is as much," said I, "as a well man can endure." I gave them some fresh papers, and they went to reading.

The field agent wanted me to preach last night. I had thought my day's work through, and told him I was too tired. He was kind, and said he would go; but he was worn down, and I went. There were about one hundred and fifty present, all soldiers.

July 19.— Have been busy as a bee. Sent three hundred dollars yesterday from various sick soldiers to their homes by

express. I have much to encourage and interest me. Many poor
sufferers are inquiring the way of salvation. Pray for a blessing
upon my labors. What a sweet thought,— that in the resurrec-
tion some may rise up from the army of the Cumberland whom I
have benefited !

A day or two ago, as I entered one of the hospital buildings, I
saw a man writhing in extreme pain, shot through both hips, and
the pain darting down his limbs. I asked: " How do you bear
your sufferings to-day? That is hard, is it not?" " Oh," says he,
" the hardest of all is that I have thrown my life away. I have
sacrificed all for nothing. It will do no good. We shall never
succeed." I was surprised; had never heard a soldier talk so
before. " Oh, no! It will be all for the best," I said. I asked
him where he was from. Found he was a rebel, from Alabama,
a noble-looking fellow, and a Christian. He seemed to have no
hope for the Confederacy; was wounded as they fell back from
Kenesaw Mountain; said God was bringing all this on us for our
sins, and that we ought to be a united nation. Poor boy ! I gave
him something to read, and left him. Many are dying. I stop at
the operating-room every day. They give chloroform, and then
cut away at the old wound, taking out gangrene. You could not
bear to look on.

On the 22d of July, he made the ascent of Lookout
Mountain, starting out early in the morning, with
breakfast in his pocket. The next day, he proceeded
to the front on a hospital train, and spent the following
two weeks with the army then laying siege to Atlanta.

In the Field, three miles from Atlanta, Ga., July 26, 1864.—
From Vining's, at the end of the railroad. we got a ride in the ambulances which had come with loads of wounded men. Some had
died on the way. After riding two miles in a choking, blinding
dust, we stopped at the Chattahooche, for the teamsters to dine.
The mules were much exhausted. After a slow ride of five or six
miles on this side of the river, we came to the hospital of the

Twentieth Army Corps, where we were cordially received. It consists of tents in the woods. All seemed clean. The patients lie on the ground. A gentle stream murmured near, in which some were bathing. We slept on the ground, amid the heavy boom of the siege-guns and the groans of the dying.

This morning, I rose early, visited some wounded rebels, and became acquainted with the medical director of the Fifteenth Corps, to which I was assigned. We started with him about ten o'clock, after helping to load the ambulances with wounded men who were going North. Proceeding a mile, we saw where Hooker had his terrible but short fight. Many new graves attested the severity of the struggle. Many Ohio boys were marked on the head-boards. The surgeon got off his horse, put on our baggage of heavy blankets, knapsacks, and canteens, and led the horse. We went to the front of our line, where I was *under fire* for the first time. A shell from a rebel battery burst in the air above us, left a little white cloud of smoke, and passed away. The sharp-shooters were but a little beyond. As we passed on, one was brought along on a stretcher wounded. You cannot imagine what strange exhilaration I felt in the excitement of a little danger,—the novelty, the booming cannon, the soldiers around us; some firing at long intervals; one reading a history of America, lying behind the breastworks. On we came to the eastward, winding here and there, to General O. O. Howard's head-quarters, where we now are with his chief commissary, Colonel David Remick,—where we have all, and abound. The cannon roar out on the night air. We expect a move to-morrow. May God prosper the right! We had a precious interview with General Howard this afternoon. He is a noble, lovely man.

July 28.—Yesterday, General Sherman commenced a flank movement toward our right, or to the west of Atlanta. The several corps to the east of us broke camp about midnight, a part reaching here soon after daylight. And of all the sights! Woods, roads, fields, far and near, full of soldiers, halted and preparing breakfast; muskets stacked, little fires built to prepare coffee and fry meat, each soldier carrying his little iron coffee-cup and spider.

The rail fences were soon used up, and soldiers busy eating pork and hard-tack. I found the Sixth and Twenty-fifth Iowa. A large number of Mount Pleasant boys gathered around me. I wrote ten letters for soldiers this morning. I wrote for one poor rebel boy, who was shot through the lungs. How he wept as he sent word to his father! He said his mother could not stand it. He was from Southern Alabama. Wagons were moving steadily all day. I never realized how much work it is to move an army. The troops formerly on the left are forming on the right. Heavy cannonading all along the line. Night and day, at short intervals, our ears are greeted with the heavy peals.

July 30.— A battle was raging on our right at the time of the cannonading. The Fifteenth Corps had been ordered to form on the right of the Sixteenth, and had just reached their position and thrown down a few logs, when the rebels were seen coming up within a few rods, in dense woods. Our men were ordered to fall behind these slight works and fire. This was the commencement of a fierce engagement of several hours, when the enemy withdrew, not having once reached our lines.

Yesterday morning, Colonel Remick asked us if we would not like to ride along the lines. As we had been working hard, we concluded to have a little rest. The colonel took his orderly to wait on us and the horses. We took a westerly direction, toward our right. The skirmishers were cracking away. Pop, pop, went the guns, and boomed the heavy cannon. We dismounted several times, and went up to the breastworks. We could see the rebel works and men walking over them.

Our forces were still passing to the right. Regiment after regiment blocked the way. There was no display. Generals walked their horses, color-bearers had their flags furled. The men kept no regular step, no music, but filed along the road, as full as it could be packed for miles. It was a grand spectacle. Those scar-worn veterans meant work. Some looked weary under their heavy knapsacks, but all marched on. We were obliged to take to the woods for a long distance in passing them, and at length

found the quarters of Brigadier-General Corse, of Burlington, who commands a division of the Sixteenth Corps. He took us to his works, showed his mounted cannon, and Atlanta through his glass. I saw the rebels standing thick on their works, about a mile away. We then went on to the Fifteenth Corps and to the battle-field, a few rods distant. It was horrible. The rebels had not been buried at this point, and lay as they fell. Nearest our works was a rebel captain, cold in death, pierced with many bullets. Just back of him lay his men. All had their clothes on, clotted with blood. Some were wounded in the head. Their clotted hair and ghastly faces presented a horrible appearance. We walked on. It was the same,— some on their faces, some on their backs. At one oak-tree, which was riddled with balls, lay two dead rebels side by side. All of them were swarming with flies. We left the sickening sight, impressed more than ever with the horrors of war. I never saw more accurate firing. Trees at about the height of four feet were completely riddled.

We now began to return. Passed the head-quarters of General Thomas. Saw him looking through his glass at the enemy's works. Also passed the head-quarters of General Sherman. Saw him reading a newspaper. We got home in a drenching rain at 5 P.M., having rode along a greater portion of the line and back again, some twenty miles.

August 2.— Yesterday, I visited the hospitals. The soldiers seemed very glad to see me. I greet them with a smile, and they almost all smile back again. They were being moved: poor, pale, legless, and armless men, without a murmur, were lifted into ambulances, to be jolted over these rough roads in the woods. We are still shifting our left or east wing to the right, wishing, by slow approaches, to reach the railroad south-west of town. Yesterday, Schofield, of the Twenty-third Corps, commenced to swing his command ten or twelve miles to our right wing. This left our hospitals exposed to the enemy. We were stopping in a house about one mile back of our fortifications. Fearing the enemy might flank us, passing round our left wing, we ran a line of

breastworks nearly north and south along the east side of the
Fourth Corps. This line struck the centre of our house. Men
came in squads, with shovels and picks and axes, and began such
a clamor. It was a novel sight to see them tear down the house.
They looked like ants running to and fro with boards and joists.
Soon it was all down,— carried away to make breastworks. The
clatter of axes was heard, cutting down trees. The rebels can
now roam where I have labored in the hospitals, nearly a mile east
of these works. I am safe in the colonel's tent, with the Fourth
Corps, formerly Howard's, now Stanley's, between me and harm.
Cannot do much to-day, everything is so stirred up.

Chattanooga, Tenn., August 10, 1864. — Back in Tennessee.
How differently I look upon everything now! The movements of
single regiments seem a small matter, and military movements
here awaken but little interest.

I held service at Marietta, Ga., on the Sabbath, in one of the
hospitals: preached or talked in three of the wards. The inmates
are continually changing, whole trains going North; but from the
fountain of sorrow and death comes a never-failing stream, which
fills up their number day after day. A tide of lusty life passes to
the front: it surges back, shattered, broken, blood-stained.

Monday, 8.— I took a few crackers for breakfast, and started to
ascend Kenesaw Mountain. Several members of the Commission
had been anxious to go, but were dissuaded on account of guerillas. I thought the risk to me alone would be small, as I trusted
to the quickness of my eye to see an enemy before he saw me.
The town was in commotion that morning. An attack was expected from Wheeler's cavalry. Spies, it was said, had entered
the city. The principal streets were barricaded, and the guards
and pickets ordered to arrest every stranger in the streets. While
in the suburbs, a lieutenant sent one of his squad for me ; but he
found me "all right," and I went on to the picket lines, but could
not go another step. Orders were stringent to pass no man whatever. So I went back to the provost-marshal. Men were being
marched in there by the scores. Among them, one of our Chris-

tian Commission men, who had charge of the rooms, came in with a bayonet behind him. I roared, as he liked to get the laugh on others, and had been afraid to go to Kenesaw, though starting twice. He said to me, "Are you caught, too?" "Oh, no! These guards can tell an honest man," I answered. I then asked the marshal for a pass, which he gave immediately.

I left, passed the pickets, and was soon in the land of desolation, silence, and death. Along the way were blackened ruins, stripped fruit-trees, corn-fields cut up, not a pig, hen, goose, or chicken. Leaving the main road, where guerillas would waylay a traveller, I plunged into the dark forests at the mountain's base. I found some lovely spots. In one place, sweet odors filled the air. The woods were filled with flowers, several varieties of which I picked, and laid away in my book for a certain lady. I started straight up the rugged side of the mountain; after some fatigue, reached the summit, where were stationed a guard of eight men. Had a beautiful view, somewhat like that at Vining's; the cannon smoke of Atlanta visible, and the reverberations fell upon the ear. Almost at my feet lay the lovely Marietta, at this distance revealing few of the desolations of war. South-east was Stone Mountain, while to the north-east my own loved Blue Ridge swept along in rugged grandeur. Lookout, peering down upon a desolated land, seemed proud to be delivered from foreign hands, and to give up its pure air and gushing fountains to recuperate the strength of the maimed heroes of liberty. The mountain-top where I stood was scarred and shattered. I followed the line of rebel breastworks for a mile and a half to the west, picked up cannon-balls, and wished I could carry them away; examined exploded shells, and where they had embedded themselves in the solid oak; saw where the battle raged hottest, and came down. Got back safely, and started at 2 P.M. for this place, where we arrived at ten o'clock next morning.

Returning from his labors for the soldiers, Mr. Pickett prosecuted his ministry at Mount Pleasant with unflagging assiduity and zeal. In the midst of

his usefulness, his life was darkened by a great sorrow,
—the sickness of his wife, and her death, June 25,
1868, leaving two little boys, John and George, to cling
the more closely to their father's guiding hand.

A year later, he was called to take the superintendence of Home Missions for Southern Iowa. The
devotion and success of his ministry had become well
known, and his zeal in evangelism marked him as peculiarly fitted for that office. At the same time, he loved
pastoral work, and the studies incumbent on one who
would feed his people with knowledge and understand-
ing; and, strong in the affections of his people, the
thought of giving up these relations, and his quiet
home and the immediate care of his children, was un-
welcome, and he demurred. Nothing moved him but
the possibilities of very great usefulness, of which the
Rev. Julius A. Reed confidently told him. He set
apart a day of fasting and prayer to consider the question and ask divine guidance: it was a day of sacred
memory,·just one year after his wife's death. On the
next day, June 26, 1869, he signified his acceptance of
the appointment, and wrote : —

I will cheerfully give up everything that would interfere with
this work, feeling that Christ can be more to me than my loved
people, that he can give me a sweeter rest than that of home, and
that he will provide for the intellectual development of those who
walk in the path of duty.

He at once provided a good home for his children at
Mount Pleasant, and removed his residence to Des
Moines, to be near the centre of his field.

CHAPTER III.

THE operations of the American Home Missionary Society in Iowa were commenced in 1836, three years after a narrow strip of its territory, "The Black Hawk Purchase," was opened to settlement. Since that period, the society has aided in planting the gospel and in sustaining new and feeble congregations in every portion of the State. All the Presbyterian churches in Iowa, formerly called "New School," and all the Congregational churches, save those at Denmark, Grinnell, Tabor, Keokuk, and Farragut, were assisted by this society in their infancy, and many of them for a series of years. In this work, the society has expended more than six hundred thousand dollars. Rev. Asa Turner, who still survives at more than fourscore to witness the fruits of his sacrifices and toils, was the first agent. It was at his call that a band of eleven ministers came to the Territory from the Theological Institution at Andover, Mass., of the class of 1843. To him succeeded Rev. Julius A. Reed, in 1845, and Rev. Jesse Guernsey, in 1858. In 1862, the field was divided into Northern and Southern Iowa, Mr. Guernsey holding the former and Mr. Reed taking charge of the latter. In November, 1864, Rev. Reuben Gaylord was called to the supervision of Western Iowa,

in conjunction with Nebraska. In addition to Mr.
Reed's district, Mr. Pickett's superintendency covered
the part of Iowa that had been under Mr. Gaylord.
He found the field full of promise. The three lines
of railway that passed through it from the Mississippi
to the Missouri were bringing multitudes to make
homes there. New towns were springing up. The
increase of population was large, especially in South-
western Iowa. He saw it to be a critical time for that
fair and fertile region, and he threw himself into the
work of establishing Christian institutions in the rising
communities. At an early period of these labors, he
wrote : —

As in loneliness and weariness I roam these rolling prairies, I
foresee some of the wonderful beauty and glory that twenty years
will unfold. Christian homes, with waving grain, teeming or-
chards, and groves from which rise church-spires, will then cover
these now untrodden solitudes. In imagination, I hear the tramp
of the coming millions who are to find homes here in the near
future, and my ardor is kindled and my footsteps quickened as I
listen to the command, —

> " Prepare ye the way of the Lord :
> Make straight in the desert a highway for our God."

For nine years, he prosecuted his work with unflagging zeal and devotion, in season and out of season,
usually preaching daily during the winter months, and
frequently visiting every family in new towns.

It is gratifying to know, he said, that we have been able to move
with this moving tide of population, and to plant in new towns and
on the broad prairies the faith and order of the Pilgrims. Yet our
work is scarcely begun. We need churches with a fervid enthusi-

asm for the truth as it is in Jesus, and many more young ministers
with glowing hearts who will know no hardships and feel no burdens, and who will move among this heterogeneous population
with a spirit so Christ-like as to win a way into every humble
cabin, whether Protestant, Catholic, or infidel, and diffuse an atmosphere of love that will draw all hearts.   I am resolved to give
all I have to enthrone Christ in this lovely State; and my greatest
joy is to welcome others to the fellowship of this labor and sacrifice.   I have foregone the enjoyments of home and family for the
sole purpose of giving myself exclusively to the work.   It is my
habit to visit the public schools as far as possible.   Passing
through the rooms with the principal, I have been invited to
make short addresses, so that I have often made half a dozen
talks on methods of study and proper preparation for life's work,
thus preparing the way for religious truth at church service.   I
have frequently held children's meetings at the close of day-
schools, having sometimes overflowing houses.   When on the
field, I have never been absent from a Sunday-school, and inva-
riably have made brief addresses.

He gave his time to weak and pastorless churches,
and especially to new towns that afforded an opening
for the planting of churches.   At Carroll, a town of five
hundred inhabitants, he held an eight days' meeting,
and visited the whole town, Catholics and all.   Some
prominent citizens were converted, and united with the
church.   Stopping one evening at Mondamin, a town
of a few hundred inhabitants on the Council Bluffs and
Sioux City road, he learned that they had no preaching.   Notice of a meeting that evening was circulated.
A crowded house awaited him; and, though but five
hours in the place, a movement was begun that re-
sulted in the formation of a church.   In his first visit
to Grand River, Adair County, after riding twelve

miles from Stuart in a farmer's wagon, he walked six miles, much of the way through heavy snow-drifts, was hungry and faint, got lost, and was almost frozen before reaching a shelter.   One starry, winter's night, he reached Cromwell, then a railroad terminus, about midnight, and, kneeling upon the frosty ground, asked God to reveal to him his work there.   When he first passed through Creston, the site contained nothing but a calf-pen.   Soon it became a division station, and the church he planted gained a leading position.   At Anita, he visited on foot all the region for miles around, and gathered members from six denominations into church fellowship.   He saw there afterward one of the most beautiful houses of worship in the State.

In prosecuting his work, he affiliated with Christians of every name, not preferring one before another, doing nothing by partiality, seeking comity and peace with all.   Reporting, 1876, the organization of six churches, he said : —

The large numbers uniting in forming these churches reveal the approach of that day long anticipated and prayed for, when Christians in our smaller towns, laying aside denominational differences, will come together on a common platform of evangelical faith.   The various denominations united with the utmost harmony, and work in perfect accord.   Houses of worship are reared, and preaching is maintained easily, and religion is honored in this unity of the body of Christ.   Our work seems clearly defined, to offer our aid to communities that wish to unite on this common platform.   We bid God-speed to all who wish to join in any other church polity; but it is believed that as many churches as can be cared for will choose to fashion their faith and order after the simplicity of our Congregational brotherhood.

I must mention one fact, not boastfully, but gratefully, in token of the good hand of my God upon me, which perhaps has not happened to another agent of the society occupying so hard a field for so long a time. In seven years of labor, I have never missed an appointment. Trains preceding or succeeding me have broken down, storms have blocked travel, bridges have been washed away; and, although hundreds of appointments have been made in different parts of the State, sometimes for weeks beforehand, Providence has so arranged that nothing has interfered with my original plans.

I have never preached a "collection sermon" since I have been in the work: not but it might have been profitable at times; but I wished to present spiritual truth, and have left this special duty to pastors. The result has been satisfactory. Contributions on my field to home missions have increased.

His heart throbbed deeply with the memories of the nation's centennial, in 1876. He visited Philadelphia with his sons, and heard the bell announce at midnight the opening of a new century. In the presence of the nations there represented, and among the exhibits of the world's advancement, the summons seemed to come to him louder than ever to guard and strengthen on his own field the moral principles and spiritual forces that underlie the peculiar civilization of America. In 1877, he wrote:—

One church has died of the dry rot of secret society and general worldliness. Proper faith and courage in the membership would have saved it. It must be regarded as a serious loss to the denomination and to the community. But, when a church resolves to die, I know of no way but to let it do so. It is not Congregational to prop up with outside help, when the inside is gone.

The only way of resisting undue denominational pressure is to maintain our churches. If, when this pressure comes, as come

it will in every community of enterprise and expectation, we throw up our hands and show our liberality by dying, we must remember that we can glorify God but once in this direction. Whereas, if we live, and stretch forth our hands across the chasms of denominational strife and selfishness, and aid in every good work, we shall commend the faith and polity of our fathers, and their principles of liberty of conscience and equality of condition and responsibility. I see and deplore more and more the corrupting tendencies of the centralized forms of church government. I am on terms of some intimacy with ministers of these denominations, and am amazed at the schemings for place and power, the ranklings and heart-burnings, among them. These are a standing demand for a polity with different tendencies.

As I look back to the time I first entered and crossed this State, I can hardly realize that this beautiful Iowa is the same land, then so wild and strange. The vast prairies of Central and Western Iowa, which appeared uninhabitable to my inexperienced eye, are now dotted with cities, farm-houses, school-houses, and churches. It is a wonderful transformation, resembling more the strangeness of fable than sober fact.

There is a great work yet to be done in this State. It may be said to have been explored. Unsurpassed in salubrity of climate, in fertility of soil, and in the beauty and sublimity of its vast rolling prairies, in the centre of the continent, in the direct line of trans-continental travel, its inhabitants noted for intelligence and morality, it is adapted to be the home of those principles of civil and religious liberty which our fathers developed.

In 1878, he wrote : —

It is forty years this May since the first Congregational Church was planted in Iowa, at Denmark. Over the whole region of Central and Western Iowa roamed the Indian. Now this vast area, dotted with cities and villages and pleasant country-homes, has become the garden of the Lord. Christians of every name have come to possess the land, and have worked in harmony side by side, till churches and school-houses adorn the landscape from

the Mississippi to the Missouri. We now have two hundred and twenty-five churches, and, at the close of these forty years of wandering and planting, are going in to possess the land with a vigor and energy greater than ever before. Although we have not developed as rapidly as some other denominations, we have reason to thank God for the strong hold secured in this Commonwealth by those churches which seem to us the representative churches of America.

During the nine years of my superintendency, Western Iowa has been rapidly settled, and is destined to become a stronghold of Congregationalism. In the valley of the Nishnabotana,—the garden-spot of the world,—we have been very successful. Of the new churches planted, scarcely one has been located where it will not be able to grow and prosper. Some have already become self-sustaining. During this period, thirty-three churches have been organized and thirty-three houses of worship dedicated. As we look into the future of this State and of these churches, we feel that, with fidelity and reliance upon God, it is to be even brighter than the past.

To help the new and struggling churches, he gave almost half of his salary, also a portion of the little patrimony that fell to him. Chided for being so large and unstinted in his gifts, nothing could repress his devotion and sacrifice. Though reducing himself to straits and debt, he felt that the opportunity was great and critical, and worthy the burdens. He rarely or never alluded to these things, but acted upon the apostolic rule, "He that giveth, let him do it with simplicity." Writing confidentially near the close of his labors in Iowa, he said : —

I saw during these years, beyond a doubt, that we were settling the condition of Congregationalism in Western Iowa for years, perhaps centuries; and I spared nothing in time, labor, sacrifice,

or money, to plant our faith and polity. We were obliged to have houses of worship. . . . I am now twelve hundred dollars in debt at bank. But the crisis is past. Railroad and town building have ceased; and I have nothing to do but pay my debts, and Western Iowa is saved to us forever.

To talk of common interests and responsibilities in his beloved circle of Iowa workers, develop efficiency in each local church, promote fellowship and co-operation, diffuse information touching every department of Christian benevolence, and help on the more rapid progress of Christ's kingdom in the State, he published annually, the last five years of his superintendency, for gratuitous distribution, a little paper, entitled *Church Work*. It was commenced at his own expense; subsequently, others helped a little in the cost; and one year the Church at Des Moines defrayed the bill. Three thousand copies of each number were circulated, with an additional eight hundred the last year. He filled it with stirring truths and facts, to awaken inquiry and stimulate enterprise and zeal in every good work. Some extracts from his articles in it, and from his other papers of this period, show his views of duty and life, and the spirit and character of his labors: —

LETTERS TO THE CHILDREN OF IOWA.

I.

HAVE A PLAN IN LIFE.

Dear Children of Iowa,— I cannot send out this paper without writing a letter to you. I know children like to get letters from their friends. I have visited many of you. I have seen some of you in your homes, and many at Sunday-school and at church. I

have visited many thousands of you in school, and have felt greatly interested in your studies.

I sometimes ask boys and girls, What are you going to do when you grow up? I find you have plans. Some expect to be teachers; some, good farmers and housekeepers; some, mechanics and merchants; some, ministers, physicians, or lawyers. I saw one boy the other day who said he was going to be a stage-driver. I think it is a good thing to have plans. A boy or a girl that has no plans will not do much in the world. I am glad to see you plan to have good lessons, to be good in school, to be always kind, never to tell a lie or swear, to be good to everybody, to study and read at home, and never miss a Sabbath at Sunday-school. Some children and some men never have plans: they float idly about all their lives, like a vessel on the ocean that is not going anywhere.

I have often thought what one plan did for me. I forget how it happened; but I made a plan, when a boy, never to sit down at home without a book or paper in my hand. I found a *History of the United States*, which I read through, and then a *History of Greece and of Rome*, and father took the New York *Tribune*. It was pretty dry sometimes; and I worked so hard on the dear old farm that I could hardly hold my head up. But my plan helped me through; and I learned about this country and all the countries in the world, which is a great help to me now. How well I remember the table in the loved home, that was brought out every night with the light on it, around which we children used to read and study! Plan to read those books which will do you the most good. I expect some of you are making plans to go away to school and to college some time. I like that. I never knew how to enjoy my home fully till I came home in vacation; and I never liked work so well as after studying hard away at school.

Now, I want you to make one more plan that will help you more than all the rest. I want you to plan to be Christians. I made this plan when a boy, and I am so happy that I have lived to carry it out.

December, 1873.

II.

HABITS.

Dear Children,— Can you tell me what a habit is ?   I think this definition will suit you : it is *the effect of doing again and again the same thing.*

Habits become stronger every time the act is repeated, till at length a character is formed ; for a good definition of character is *the sum of all our habits.*   So, if I want to know your character, all I have to do is to add your habits together, and I can tell what kind of men and women you are to be.

A boy forms a habit of swearing.   That habit will get stronger every time he repeats it, until he will swear without knowing it ; and he will be led into bad company, and be ruined at last, because he formed a bad habit when a boy.   There is a boy or a girl that begins to tell little white lies at home or at school.   They look so small that you think little of them.   But they are the harmless egg of the serpent, which will hatch out the deadly adder to poison your life, and drive away from you the beautiful angel of truth.   I see small boys forming a habit of chewing tobacco or smoking cigars.   I think what an evil practice they are pinning to their lives, how much money they will waste that might be employed in doing good.   I see other boys taking a glass of beer. They say, " This is nothing : just beer."   Poor boys, I could weep for you !   I see such sorrow, wretchedness, and misery in the future.   Oh, that terrible habit !   How gently it begins !   How harmless at first !   I see others who have a habit of breaking the Sabbath.   When Sunday comes, they are restless, and go loafing and lounging.   Many men in the State prison to-day say they began a life of wickedness by Sabbath-breaking.

Some boys and girls form the habit of being kind and pleasant to every one ; and it comes easy when they grow up.   Others are cross and unkind, and form a habit of scolding and fretting ; and they have trouble with this habit all their lives.

Some parents give their children a calf or lamb or other property, and tell them they can get rich, and have many things.

These children grow up with this thought: they live for themselves alone, and think of nothing else. They will not give for the Sunday-school or for any good cause; but their hearts become smaller and smaller as they love money more than Christ, and at last they become misers. When I came through Kansas last summer, on my way from Colorado, I spent my Sabbath with a college professor. I went out to his garden, which was all eaten up by the grasshoppers, and his little boys showed me two rows of sweet potatoes they had planted, which they were going to dig and sell, and send the money to missionaries to the heathen. But the grasshoppers had completely ruined them; and, as the boys and the father looked upon the rows for the heathen children, they seemed to feel worse about them than for the rest of the garden. Those boys were forming habits of working for others, which will make them like Jesus.

I must tell you a story I heard the other day: Two boys, James and John, formed the habit of reading about the heathen, and giving money to help save them. When they grew up to be almost men, John said: "Somebody must go to tell the heathen about Jesus. Ought not we to go?" James said, "We have to work on the farm, and take care of father and mother, who are growing old; and we have not money to go to college and become missionaries." John said, "That is so." But a great and noble thought came to James. "I have it," he said: "I will stay at home and work hard, and take care of father and mother, and earn money enough to send you to college, and then to the heathen." "I will go," said John. So he went to college and studied hard, and James stayed at home and worked, and saved all he could, and father and mother helped, too; and John went through college, and then far across the ocean to the heathen, and James supported him all the way. Now, which do you think was the missionary, James or John? "Both of them," you say. That is so; and father and mother, too. I love to think what a happy family they were in the dear home, as they read John's letters about the heathen, and felt they were all helping. Yes; and, when they get to heaven, I think they will be happy to meet John and the

heathen he has brought with him. Will not Jesus join that circle, as they tell how they labored and prayed and sacrificed for him on earth, and tried to walk in his steps? Will it not be worth more than all the selfish pleasure they could have had in this world, to hear him say, "Well done"?

Now, boys and girls, I want you to form habits of reading about missionaries and helping their work. That will make you missionaries. Some of you will go, and some will stay and work hard to support the rest. Yes, James and John and Charley, all of you; and the girls, too, Lizzie and Jennie and Mary,—it would take a great deal of paper to call all your names,—we want you to form these habits of being like Jesus, and doing good. I know that the best thing we can do is to try and help this world to be better. Do you find it hard sometimes to be good? Yes, Jesus knew you would, and came from heaven on purpose to help us. Let me tell you of one more habit which will be a great blessing to you,—the habit of coming to Jesus every day in prayer, and of feeling that your life is united with his. This will be worth more than all the world.

January, 1875.

III.

EVERY CHILD TO DO HIS DUTY. — MIND, MORALS, AND RELIGION
TO BE CULTIVATED.

Dear Children,— One hundred years since, our fathers fought to make us free and happy, marking with blood from their bare feet the frozen ground on which they marched, because the nation was too poor to buy a few thousand pairs of shoes. We shall not forget them; and we shall often ask, What can I do to make the nation still greater and better?

I find that every one who does good in the world asks that question. Well-doing does not come, like wild fruit, without cultivation. It takes resolution and perseverance to be good and to do good. When the gallant Nelson fought the great naval battle with France, he hung up at the mast-head of his flag-ship the

words, "England expects every man to do his duty." Those
words may have gained for England that victory. So, my young
friends, I think the best thing for you to do is to hang up over the
unwritten page of this year this motto : "God expects every boy
and girl to do their duty."

You do not want this year covered with blots ; and it will be, if
you do not try to prevent it. A hard fight we all have with wrong
and temptation; and we shall have to look at the flag-ship a good
many times, if we are not overcome. You want a great deal of
pleasure this year, and that you cannot have, unless you are a hard
worker. Then, when you have a play-day, you will enjoy it, but
not without. The idler can never be happy.

I will say a few things to put on your fingers to remember.
1. *Your minds must be cultivated.* This is what you are in
school for. But only a few persons have cultivated minds. It is
only the thinkers and those who love to think hard that are benefited. I can tell the hard thinkers. They read useful books and
papers, and talk about what they read, and think of it when by
themselves, and plan to make study useful.

You have a good religious paper for family reading, and a children's paper for the smaller ones. What a blessing this is in
your home ! Talk with father and mother about what you read.
It will do them good. It will do you good. When you find what
you think will do you good, treasure it up, or have a book to
write it in. I was looking over my old blank-books the other
day, where I wrote many years ago things worth remembering.

2. Here is for your second finger. *Your morals must be cultivated.* We all have a work in this direction. I saw one of the
best girls in this State crying as if her heart would break. She
threw her arms around an elder sister's neck, and whispered.
After she had gone away, I asked the elder sister what she said.
The reply was, " It is so hard to be good." I thought, if that girl
finds it hard to be good, what will become of the rest of us ? I
saw that she had become good *by hard trying every day*.

Look at that boy who swears. I feel sorry for him, and I
always speak to him about it. He sometimes laughs, and runs

off. But, if every one would make that rule, there would be less swearing. Then, there is the boy or girl that tells lies. I feel sorry for them, too. They go to school to get good, and destroy it by this bad habit. Let this be a year of truthfulness. The boy that uses tobacco, I feel sorry for. He smokes cigars, and burns away in a few days enough to buy him a good book or a paper for the family. · I have been expecting to see this habit broken up ; but its practice, after physicians and educators tell us it is injurious, shows how weak moral principle is in our young men. My young friends, this is a good year to begin with firmness as to these poisons to soul and body.

3. Here I have a beautiful, sparkling ring for your third finger. I hope you will wear it all the year : yes, and you may keep it on always. It will not break nor wear out. *Resolve this year to be a bright, happy, and useful Christian.* This precious privilege is worth all else. You and I can never thank God enough for the gift of his Son, to wash away every thing dark and bad from our hearts, and give us every thing bright and good. We do not think of this enough. You must ask somebody to tell you the story of Joseph Neesima, the Japanese boy, who ran away from home, that he might come to America and learn about Jesus, and how God led him, and he became a missionary. It is a grand story. They call me a home missionary, because I go around among our churches and try to do them good. But I want to call you a home missionary, because you make home bright and beautiful with goodness, and your neighbor's home happy with your presence. Some of you will become Christians, and unite with the church this year; so it will be the best year of your life. So wear this ring, and you will have ornaments enough.

Now, let me look at your hand once more. Yes, I see. There is the first finger, which tells you to care for your mind, and the second for your morals, and the third for the religion of Jesus, to help all the rest. And now, with one more good look at the flagship, we will go out to the duties of the year.

January, 1876.

IV.

PRAYER-TRIANGLES.— LIFE A COPY-BOOK.

Dear Children,— Happy New Year to all! I know you are looking for this greeting, which has come to you for three years. I called the other day at a home in Western Iowa, when a little girl ran to the bookcase and brought my last year's paper, telling me how much she had enjoyed my letter. How I should like to see you all this bright morning! But, next to seeing friends, is writing to them. I should like to welcome you to my pleasant office in Des Moines. From this quiet room has gone forth much thought and feeling and prayer for our beautiful Iowa, and many wishes for you, that you may be noble and true, and do great good in the world. Here I have made a great many prayer-triangles to every place where this paper will go.

You ask: " What do you mean? Tell me what prayer-triangles are." You know a triangle is a figure with three sides. One is the line of thought between me and you; the second is the thought I lift to God for you; and the third is the blessing from God to you. Along that line, I have often felt that some blessings were coming down. Yes; and, when God sent the blessing, he did not forget the other line. He also sent joy to me; and then the line between us seemed to thrill so sweetly.

Do you know that along these lines God sends almost all the spiritual blessings that come to this world? Perhaps no one is converted without some one praying for him. Thus God works through these triangles. Think how many of them we can make, — for father and mother, for brother and sister, for your minister and teacher, for your church and Sabbath-school, for your town, for our State and country, for the world, for our missionaries,— that the heathen may listen to the story about Jesus, who loved us and gave himself for us.

But I must not talk longer about this beautiful triangle. I wonder if you will understand it. Ah! here comes from his cosey bed my twelve-year-old visitor from Mount Pleasant with " A happy New Year!" He shall hear what I have written. . . . He

says: " I never thought of that before. It is beautiful, papa; and the triangle is a *right-angle triangle*." Yes, I see you understand it, for children have better teachers now than the older people had. May we learn how to use it morning and evening, and through the day! Then life will be happy and pure, and every bitter fountain will be turned into sweetness.

Not yet light! This is an early talk; but the printers are waiting, and this letter must reach you this week. How beautiful the morning! Not a cloud in the sky, only the stars and the moon, bright and clear. The shadows of the naked trees lie about my window on the white snow, pure and clean as the unwritten page of the new year upon which you and I are just beginning to write.

Life has been compared to a copy-book, neat and clean when you buy it. There is the white paper with its straight lines, and a beautiful copy at the top. Your life and mine is that copy-book. Each page is a year, each line is a day. The lines are *the laws of right*, and the copy is JESUS OUR SAVIOUR. Now we all begin to write. You will have written a few lines before this reaches you. There are two things we will try to do,—keep the line, and write as near like the copy as we can. Write with a steady hand. Lift up your eye to the copy often. That is the secret of life. Now, let us try to make this our best year on earth,—the year to study the hardest, work most faithfully, speak kindest words, do noblest deeds, love the most. Look out! That habit will bring you below the line. The line is the Commandment:—

" Thou shalt not."
" Remember."
" Honor."

Do the lines of the year seem many? Soon they will all be written. But some of us may stop in the middle of the page, and in the middle of the line, and the rest will remain unwritten for-ever. I heard yesterday that Mr. P. P. Bliss, your sweet singer, had been killed by a terrible railroad accident. His songs seemed sweeter than ever, as we thought of him singing the songs of heaven. Shall we sing with him " the new song," and with Jesus,

our greater Leader? How many of you will become Christians
this year, and give your life to doing good?

Well, my letter is again long. The morning sun is throwing his
first rays over the grand walls of the new Capitol, and I will throw
a good-by to you all. *Make the triangles; remember the bright
page; keep the line; look to the copy.*

January, 1877.

V.

GOODNESS.

Dear Children,— I think I have never enjoyed trying to do
good so much as during the past year. Is there anything that
makes us so happy? How bright it makes the world and the
heavens! I have been looking at the stars a good deal lately,— so
many that we cannot count them, and so far away that we cannot
measure the distance. Yet God made all these; and how strong
and wise and good he must be! I look at the glow of early morning and the brightness of evening, and I cannot help thinking of
God in everything. Is it not sweet to have the thought of him in
all we see and hear and know? I visited a home a few days since.
A little friend said, " Our rose is in blossom on purpose for you."
It was fragrant and beautiful in its rich purple dress. How could
I help feeling thankful to God in my heart?

When I look upon your house-plants, and see the delicate ivy
climbing along so carefully, and geraniums of various hues, and
verbenas and pinks and fuchsias, and how God has made each
leaf and stalk and flower out of the same dark earth, I say in my
heart, Our God is a wonder-working God. Yes; and next spring
we shall walk out into God's great world-house, and see what he
has made there. Every leaf and flower, every tree and blade of
grass, speak of his goodness and love. I have scarcely ever
walked in the beautiful woods alone, since a boy, without kneeling
down to thank God for all his goodness. The woods, the groves
about your house, seem like God's church that he built for us to
worship in. I love to enter them and listen to the winds murmur-
ing through the leaves. It seems like God's great organ, sounding

sweetly of his love. I do not wonder that all Israel, when they came up to their beautiful temple, used to chant in a great chorus:

> "Oh, give thanks unto the Lord:
> For he is good; his mercy endureth forever."

I think we shall all say, I had rather have a thankful heart than everything else in this world.

I got a letter from the deacon of a church last week. He said, "We have no pastor, and we want you to come and receive a number of our children into the church." That made me feel very happy,—to think the children were finding Jesus, even without a pastor. Yes, Jesus is not hard to find, when we seek him with the whole heart. We shall all find it the happiest life to take him as our Saviour, and do good and be useful.

With much love, I remain your friend,

‑ J. W. PICKETT.

January, 1878.

THE PAST, PRESENT, AND FUTURE OF IOWA.

It is now forty years since the first settlement was made (June 1, 1833). Our development for a time was slow. Indian titles were but just extinguished; the vast, untrodden prairies were shunned by settlers of the well-wooded East; the early inhabitants clung to the timbered watercourses and patches of woodland. They little dreamed of the throbbing life soon to sweep over those solitudes.

Within a few years, all is changed. Trade, with its swift instincts, has found highways through these fertile prairies for spanning the continent, and bears to us the wealth and population of the nations. From Germany, Scandinavia, England, and all parts of our country, an increasing tide is sweeping in upon us.

In the southern half of the State, more than one hundred churches of our faith and order have been planted. What is to be their future, and their influence upon the future of the State,

of Christianity, and of the world? If we have not misapprehended, there is with many something of the purpose that actuated the Pilgrim Fathers,— to plant institutions and a Christian State which shall reflect more perfectly the image of Christ. They feel that the highest work of life is to develop a Christian civilization, and give themselves, their property, and their all for the moral regeneration of the world. It may require a vision like that of Abraham to span the coming centuries, but God will give it to them that ask him.

There is a grand and an almost awful meaning in the fact that this beautiful and fertile section of the world was left unoccupied by civilized man through the ages, and is thrown open for us to occupy at such a time as this. Why were all its secret treasures hidden from the cupidity of the nations, now to be flung open to all people in this period of the world's grandest possibilities?

Our State is passing to a period of responsible manhood. We take our position in the world for good or evil. It is a critical period with a State, as with an individual, when its life comes in contact with the world. That is our position to-day. As Christians, we must not become absorbed in farms, shops, and household cares, when the world's mighty voices are ringing in our ears. We must feel that these things are but means to ends. We must stand on the watch-tower of consecration and service, and ask, "What wilt thou have me to do?" It is possible that we have been called to lay the foundations of a higher type of piety than the world now enjoys, to cultivate a truer Christian simplicity in thought and manner of living, to develop wealth for the grand consummation of the world's conversion. If so, what joy and peace will come to us with this object ever in view! How pleasant sacrifice will become, as this mission opens with widening prospect! How our children's hearts will thrill with these conceptions, and what enduring legacies will we leave them in thoughts of sacrifice for others, and of fidelity to God, while worldly fortunes shrivel in financial disaster!

December, 1873.

WEAKNESS IN CHURCHES.

1. A church may shrink from the sacrifice demanded in providing a suitable place of worship; or the house may be partially completed, with a heavy debt, and no strenuous efforts to cancel it; or it may be unfit for worship by negligence. Sometimes a week's labor of the pastor is lost by failure of the sexton to build a fire in season, or from having no sexton, and leaving the first comer to do the work, amid shivering children and anxious parents; or an old stove and uncleaned pipe or chimney fills the house with smoke, so that the service becomes an agony, and the worshipper rushes from his place of confinement, performing at least one act of devotion as he thanks God for the pure air and clear sky. Are these small things? But such things give success or failure.

2. The pastor's salary may be unpaid when due. Churches guilty of this cannot realize the anxiety and injury produced by this neglect. You have secured a pastor, and promised to pay him each quarter. The term expires. The church of the covenant-keeping God has broken its promise. The pastor is in want. But often less endurable than want and suffering is the thought that the church is indifferent to its pledges, and not in sympathy with its pastor. Dear brother, would you strengthen your church, see that on the day your pastor's salary is due it is paid, every cent. The Israelite was blessed in giving to God the first-fruits of his increase. He was not to taste of bread or parched corn or green ears till he had brought an offering to God.

But we cannot meet this obligation, you say. The words *can* and *cannot* will change their meaning before the millennium. A follower of Christ *can* do some things, if necessity requires. He can give up tobacco, tea, coffee, sugar; he can do without carpets; he can dispense with many comforts which it is pleasant to have. But he *cannot* afford to break one pledge that he makes for Christ's kingdom. Do you desire to strengthen your pastor in his sermons, to cheer him in the closet, to sweeten his visitations from house to house, to give efficiency to all his labors? Keep your pledges of support to the letter. Better walk through the worst

Iowa mud five miles to church meeting than violate a pledge one hour. Let the church be an embodied conscience, and in its business teach the world the beauty and power of truth and personal integrity.

3. Look into the prayer-meeting. How many of the members are present, and who are they? If the good deacons and Sunday-school workers feel the necessity of the place of prayer to renew their strength, how must the case stand with you who are not active in Christian work, and are covered with the dust of business and worldly care? Why are you not there? Are you detained by business, pleasure, weariness, or other engagements? May not these excuses dishonor Christ?

The same inquiries might be made respecting Sunday-school work, and the extra meetings of the church, often necessary for its spiritual growth. It may be found that weakness has come through neglect in these, which you have thought small, matters.

4. We mention one more cause of weakness,—discord among brethren. We cannot express our anguish as we have seen Christ thus wounded in the house of his friends. There are churches dismantled, houses of worship falling to decay, their tottering spires pointing to heaven in silent protest against the spirit of strife which has eaten like a cancer. But the blame is with the other party. Yes, we know that. We also feel sure that, if you realized the crime you are committing against religion, against the Saviour who died, yea, against your own soul, you would never leave your closet till these divisions are melted in the crucible of love. Persons think so differently that I have resolved, for the sake of peace, to go three-fourths of the way; for, if each is only willing to go half-way, neither will come quite to the line, and their hands will not touch.

December, 1873.

_____

PROVIDE THINGS HONEST.

One hindrance to the growth of our churches is the laxness in business habits of a portion of the members. They cannot enter

upon systematic beneficence, because they have nothing to lay by in store on the first day of the week, though having means of acquiring wealth such as the world never before furnished. They incur debts on every hand,— store-bills, grocer's, butcher's. They have nothing to pay till their crops come in, and then their lump is devoured by half-famished creditors in a moment. In these wasteful methods, their word is forgotten, promises are straws, broken at a touch, and men's consciences are debauched. Our ministers suffer perplexity and embarrassment from these unchristian ways. Men belonging to the church have given their promises, and then with those promises broken look their minister in the face for a whole hour every Sunday morning without wincing. Do we wonder that churches remain unblest, with this hardening process going on ?

You ask: " What shall we do ? We are in debt, and likely to be for some time." Call a solemn family council. Let husband, wife, and children concur that the first work is to free yourselves from debt, from this bondage of corruption. Deny yourselves every luxury; live with strict economy; give up every bad or expensive habit. Do not ask what you need, but what you can do without, and let this decide every purchase till you are a *free man.* Then pay as you go, value for value. And banish what the world calls high life, the idea of rivalling your neighbor in dress or equipage. It is a snare and delusion, that ends in mortification. A man who conscientiously starts out with the resolve to keep every promise will be helped of God to do so.

1875.

DENOMINATIONAL COMITY.

The world is moving in the line of Christian Brotherhood. Various denominations are realizing that they are not antagonistic elements, to rejoice over each other's discomfiture, but one body in Christ, and members one of another. In the midst of these

signs of promise, the condition of churches in small towns is attracting attention, and Christians are beginning to wonder why a half dozen weak and sickly churches have been planted where one or two could accomplish the work better, and relieve ministers and means for regions beyond. A feeble, inefficient church does not commend religion to the world, nor honor God, nor inspire satisfaction and peace in his service. It is believed that our small churches in this State are cultivating a spirit of brotherly love toward all Christians, and are ready to engage in any union work which will advance the cause of Christ. We say to them, You have been receiving missionary money for years, and naturally ask what should be done as to organic union with other denominations. It is doubtless your duty to inquire whether you have a special work to do in your community, which on the whole will honor Christ in the way you are doing it more than in any other. The time is at hand when the church that has no mission should yield to one that has. If you cannot be *hot* in the pursuit of righteousness and in saving the perishing, the Saviour has told us it were better to be *cold.* This ought to settle the matter of life or death. If you are not willing to make sacrifices, if no souls are saved, if there is general apathy, unless this can speedily change, we cannot see as Christ gives you a right to live.

On the other hand, if there are a few earnest believers who feel after prayerful investigation that they can advance the cause of Christ more rapidly by uniting with some other Christian body, it is their duty to do so. We are not afraid to give such advice; for the denomination that most honors Christ, and will permit nothing to stand between him and a perishing world, will be most honored of him.

January, 1875.

_____

CONGREGATIONAL ORDER ADAPTED TO UNITE NEW COMMUNITIES.

Four churches were organized in 1875 : at Mount Hope, Davis County, with twenty members; Pilgrim Church in Union County,

with eighteen; at Farragut, with thirty-five; and Warren Township, with thirty. Those familiar with the number usually uniting in the formation of a church will be surprised to see so many coming into one organization in these places. This is the realization of a hope long entertained, that it would in time be seen that Congregational churches possess facilities for uniting all the Christian element of our small towns, which are not possessed by any other body.

The organization of these churches, and of many others in Southern Iowa, within the past few years, on a union basis, is a proof that these hopes are not delusive. These churches were organized by the union of Christians of some six different denominations, who saw the gain that must accrue by joining forces for the support of a regular pastor, instead of having only scattering, occasional preaching. It is believed that, where there is no interference by ministers of any denomination, Christians will thus come together as naturally as drops of water. This opinion is demonstrated by facts every year.

The Congregational polity is adapted above all others to our incoming population. No denomination has such facilities for planting the gospel in new communities as a Congregational Church. We believe that the Saviour committed all power to the local church, and hesitate to delegate this trust to any other body. A disregard of this principle opened the way for that abuse of power which has darkened the annals of the Church from the fourth century. We have a standard of equal rights and of Christian belief, upon which all Christians can unite without compromising any fundamental principle.

Brethren of other ecclesiastical systems say: " We can find no fault with you, as far as you go. We confess that your churches have possessed great power in moulding the educational, civil, and religious institutions of our country, and that they harmonize with liberty." Others say, " If I had a church of my own, I should prefer it; but I see no reasons why, in such a community as this, I should separate myself from you, because we differ respecting an external ordinance." Now, is this practical com-

mon-sense or not ? Is this view of religion to gain or to lose ground ?

The whole Christian community in the thriving young town of Farragut came together in the recent organization, without consultation with any minister, refusing to be pulled to pieces by conflicting denominational interests. All came together as one in Christ, to regulate their own affairs, choose and support their minister, and build their house of worship. But trials await them. Zealous ministers of various denominations may leave the fields where souls are perishing, and pry out a stone here and there from this temple to form little organizations, where missionary money can be bestowed, and the steady work of a settled pastor be exchanged for scattered visits and precarious labors by those who cannot prosecute a course of Christian teaching and pastoral supervision, such as made the homes of New England centres of the best influences that have swayed the minds of men.
1876.

CONGREGATIONAL ORDER AND SECTARIANISM.

If any Christians should have exalted views of the Church, it is the Congregational body. A fear is expressed by some of the New England fathers that we are becoming sectarian as a denomination. We who have passed among the Congregational churches of the West know that this is not the case. Our polity, our broad, evangelical faith, are necessarily undenominational. But there is a settled and strengthening determination to maintain our churches as an antidote against sectarian zeal and denominational aggrandizement. Shall we, when sectarian strife wages around our unwalled Zion, yield to the raging elements, and withdraw? This would be a magnanimity second only to that which refused to plant our churches at all. No : where intense sectarianism develops itself, there the cause of Christ demands of us a firm and determined stand. With our evangelical faith as broad and a

polity as simple as the gospel, we are to stretch our hands across denominational barriers, and plead for harmony and fellowship. We have no "ism" to maintain, but a broad catholicity. We are linked to no ponderous courts of judicature, which may drag us from our gospel moorings. We have no Babel of ecclesiasticism that we are bound to rear to the heavens. I have yet to find the first Congregational Church in Iowa that is not known for liberality toward all Christians, and willingness to co-operate in every good work. Nothing but a pure love for souls can win the better class of our communities to Christ. We have yet to show that the local church as an organism born of God, complete in itself, looking to Jesus as its Head and to the Word of God as its rule, moving freely under the guidance of the Spirit, and drawing and assimilating all that is capable of being used in the spiritual temple, is the mightiest power for the moral rectification of the world. This faith, and courage to assert it, is all that is needed to organize victory. This will find important work to be done in the vicinity of every church, will give a hundred hands to do it, and will thus plant the germ of many future churches. When pastors and churches plan their work along every line of Christian activity, and the entire membership resolve to carry out those plans, then the golden age of Christianity will have dawned.

TO HIS MOTHER, ON HIS FORTY-FOURTH BIRTHDAY.

The morning is beginning to dawn as I sit in the quiet of my pleasant room to meditate on the past. I have just awakened from a pleasant dream of the olden time. I was in the old sugar-camp, kindling the morning fire; and I awoke to contemplate the rolling years and the changes time has wrought. I am forty-four, and must face the fact that a good share of life is gone. I can say that goodness and mercy have followed me all my days. Through the good hand of my God upon me, there has been no

disappointment in my life-work. He has made my ways to prosper. With my staff, I crossed this Jordan into this wild but beautiful land, and he has made me two bands. My Rachel is buried in the land of my pilgrimage; but the son of my right hand God has watched over, and made him a comfort to me. He shall not be called Benoni.

My one thought and desire is to abide under the shadow of the Almighty, that the power of Christ may rest upon me. I want to do the will of God completely, walking in all his ways and commandments blameless. Personal ambition has mostly passed away. It seems to me that God could have raised up another to have done this work as well as I, and that it will not occasion the least jar in his plans to dispense with me at any time and put another in my place. That he may work, without any hindrance on my part, whatever he has to accomplish through me, is my entire wish.

But the light is dawning brighter, and I must close. I am very thankful that God has spared you so long, after a life of such toil and hardship. Your daily prayers have walked these prairies and planted these thirty-five churches, whose light breaks their vastnesses.

Des Moines, Jan. 28, 1876.

A CHURCH ENLARGED.

Some of our churches are coming to the conviction that spiritual enlargement is within their grasp,—that they have only to reach forth with faith and courage, in order to possess great spoils of Satan's kingdom. I will mention one church that has acted upon this conviction. Other cases are as remarkable. I was called, a few days since, to the dedication of a house of worship at Dunlap, a new town, a division-station on the North-western Railroad. One year ago, the Congregational Church in this pleasant village possessed a small edifice, poorly constructed, smoky and dingy, in the suburbs of the town, and inconvenient of access. A small

congregation worshipped here, that had struggled for some years amid conscious poverty and more or less divisions. A year since there came to this people a strong desire for the spirit of God. Meetings were held, with marvellous results. This sceptical town was revolutionized by the Spirit. Merchants, bankers, leading men, were converted. The strength of the two churches, Methodist and Congregational, was doubled. Our people said, "Let us arise and build." A subscription paper was circulated. Hard times were forgotten, men's poverty disappeared. One man gave six hundred dollars. Others of the new converts gave hundreds each. The most eligible site in the town was chosen, and a number of lots were purchased. The result is a beautiful house of worship, costing some four thousand dollars, with audience-room, prayer-room, and minister's study on the same floor, opening together, and presenting an attractive appearance. And all was accomplished without aid from the Union, without debt, or collection on dedication day. Reaching there after dark on the evening before dedication, the guests were ushered into the audience-room, and welcomed by a large assembly. The chandeliers were brightly burning. Baskets of trailing vines were pendent from the walls. Calla lilies and other flowers adorned the choir and pulpit. The view to one whose last visit had been to the old church was enchanting.

The next morning at six o'clock, the bell called to prayer. The morning was of surpassing loveliness. The light broke clear and beautiful over the vast rolling prairies. The morning star seemed to beam upon one object that drew all eyes. It was our first view of the exterior of the church. The spire and pinnacles rising from the fair structure, the central object in this romantic town, revealed one of the most tasteful churches in Western Iowa. The prayer-meeting, well attended, was followed by a fellowship-meeting at ten, the dedication services at two P.M., and preaching in the evening. The next day, similar meetings were held, communion taking the place of the dedicatory service. I cannot describe the joy and enthusiasm that attended these services.

With a bound, the church has sprung into life. Old difficulties

have passed away. Warm love for Christ and each other seems to characterize the whole body. Each member bears the mantle of a broad, Christian charity, and the church is becoming a busy workshop for Christ. Is this anything more than the power of his religion and the normal condition of a body of true believers?
1876.

THE IMPORTANCE OF SYSTEMATIC GIVING.

Neither the calls for increasing liberality nor the true conception of Christian giving can be satisfied through the present method of raising funds for religious purposes. Look at the

Demands for Increasing Liberality.

In our own land, immigration is setting westward, so as to move the centre of population for the nation five miles each year along fifteen hundred miles of longitude, peopling an area equal to Massachusetts. Into this region are pressing the evil and the good, the drinking-saloon and the gambling-house contending with the church and the school-house. In every town and village, this contest is being waged; and the right is hampered by lack of means to carry forward Christian enterprises.

Now is the golden moment for the freedmen of the South. Our appliances for giving a Christian education to this class of our countrymen reveal the hand of God in preparing us for a work of immense extent among them. But at this crisis the means are wanting to do that work.

To-day, the gates of opportunity are open wide throughout the earth, and the Church is invited to enter. Yet we are forced to listen to that pitiful cry of "retrenchment" from the American Board, which has carried sadness to missionary stations in all parts of the heathen world.

Among ourselves, ministerial labor and all Christian enterprise are hampered by inadequate support. Every device that ingenuity

can contrive has been resorted to for raising funds. Appeals to pleasure, to pride, to the stomach, to chance, to almost every prejudice and passion, have been made, until the work of raising money for Christ's kingdom has become so rasping to sensitive persons that they will undertake it only under pressure of conscience or dire necessity. It is intimated that this continual appeal to worried and exhausted sensibilities cannot longer accomplish even partial results. An English writer thinks that reaction has already set in, and that there is danger of serious diminution in the receipts of benevolent societies.·

Limits of Ability to Give.

We hear the statement made on every hand, "We cannot do more." Is this so? Let us glance at the contributions of our denomination. For home and foreign missions and the freedmen, we give somewhat more than a million of dollars; and for other objects, another million. For home expenses, we may estimate five millions more, making a total of seven millions. The amount raised by all denominations in our country for the support and spread of the gospel is nearly fifty millions. Compare this with amounts expended in some other directions.

Dr. Young, chief of the Bureau of Statistics, gives the estimated cost of intoxicating liquors consumed in the United States in a single year at seven hundred and thirty-five millions of dollars, almost fifteen times the amount given by all the churches of Christ in the land for the establishment and extension of his kingdom. We look with pride at what our State has done for the establishment of that kingdom within our borders. All the denominations give something over a million of dollars each year for religious purposes. But Iowa expends in a single year for intoxicating liquors fifteen million and three hundred and sixty-five thousand dollars, more than ten times the amount given for all religious purposes. Can the most unthrifty class of our population give such sums without a murmur to gratify a degrading appetite? And will Christians, who profess to see the coming of the Lord in the movements of our times, do no more for the salva-

tion of a world ? Is it possible that our churches are paying more
for single articles of luxury than for the maintenance of religion?
We come to the conclusion which all arrive at who have investi-
gated this subject,—that we have scarcely touched the borders
of our capabilities.

The Only Adequate Motive.

How, then, shall we meet the demands of the hour? Shall we
strive to make more vivid appeals? Shall ministers on each recurring year try to outdo themselves in gathering startling facts,
and in pressing truth home, until, in some excited moment, men
unclasp the purse before Mammon is aware of it? Shall we look
for a wave of enthusiasm to sweep over the world, leading the
churches to lay a richer offering on the altar? But tidal waves
ebb, and there is no sure dependence here. There is a growing
conviction that our failure has been one of method,— that we have
been giving to various "causes," and have left out of sight the
Supreme Cause. We have been looking at inferior reasons, and
forgotten the highest motive that can appeal to the soul,— *obligation to God.*

The only thing that can save us, under our absorbing contact
with sensuous objects, from gross materialism, is a pervading
sense of our stewardship in the use of this world. That beautiful
refrain of the Hebrews,

> " The earth is the Lord's,
> And the fulness thereof,"

must sound along the line of our daily avocations. God has leased
this world to us for a term of years, and said,—

> "Occupy till I come."

He claims a portion of all our earnings. As his steward, I have
no right to use a farthing till I have reckoned with him and given
him his just dues. Our gifts are to be the direct offering to God
of a fixed portion of our income as an act of worship. Giving
thus becomes lodged at the heart of the Christian life. It seems
strange that the Christian world should have departed from this

primal religious conception, and lost the sweetness and power of the words of Jesus: —

"It is more blessed to give than to receive."

This, and this alone, must prove the solution of the vexed question, and put a stop to those unworthy motives and commercial methods which have pervaded our Christian liberality.

A Law Older than Moses.

This giving of a definite portion of our earnings to God antedates the ceremonial law by hundreds of years, and probably was established from the beginning by divine command, together with the Sabbath day. The sacrifices of Cain and Abel were made in accordance with an established system. Abram, returning from the slaughter of the kings, would take no spoils to himself, "not from a thread to a shoe-latchet," yet acknowledged God's right to all, paying tithes to Melchisedec, the type of Christ. At that supreme moment in the life of Jacob, when the heavens opened, and the world of faith dawned upon him, he lifted up a pillar, and made a vow: "If God will be with me in the way that I shall go, then the Lord shall be my God, and of all that thou shalt give me I will surely give the tenth unto thee." In the Jewish law of tithes, the occasion and motive for these gifts are not stated, after our modern methods, as in the necessities of the priests and the temple service, but in this,— "that thou mayest learn to fear the Lord thy God." And the priests were commanded to give, that they, too, might share in the acknowledgment of these supreme obligations.

When the Jews wandered from God and neglected the weightier duties of the law, Christ reproved their hypocrisy, but declares of their tithing, even of garden-seeds: "This ought ye to have done, and not to leave the other undone." Throughout the word of God, giving from a pure heart, though out of the depths of poverty, is commended. The poor widow that cast into the treasury all her living was not impoverished, for He who stands over against the treasury saw her gift of love and knew her every need.

There are deeds that speak louder than any word of prayer or praise. The alabaster box of precious ointment not only filled the room where Jesus was with fragrance, but has filled the world for eighteen hundred years with the odor of a consecrated act. Paul exhorts poverty-stricken disciples to labor with their hands, that they may have to give to him that needeth. The moment one begins to give from pure motives, his life is transfigured: he joins the benefactors of his race.

A Definite Portion.

It is becoming more and more evident that setting apart a definite amount as a sacred portion for the Master's use is the starting-point of a revolution in the Church,—an antidote against extravagance on one hand and hoarding on the other. The Jew called the tithe the hedge around the rest of his property. Can one doubt the wholesome effect upon himself of having all his earnings thus pass under the eye of God?

Is it asked, How much shall each disciple give? We answer, A definite portion, determined beforehand with thought and prayer. With this decision, let there be faith in the promises, a conviction that no man can give of his earnings, on the ground that "the Master hath need," who shall not in some way "receive an hundred-fold in this present time, and in the world to come life everlasting." In determining the amount to be given, remember that where much is given much will be required; remember the land we possess, our means for developing wealth, the "unspeakable gift" we have received, and the demands of God upon his Church. In view of greater light, greater opportunities, and greater exhibitions of goodness and love, few will set apart less than one-tenth; while many, with grateful Zaccheus, will give one-half, or, in emergencies like those of the early Church, will lay everything at the apostles' feet.

Objections.

It may be objected that this is binding us to the rigidity of law, to strict rules and arithmetical calculation. One says, "The gospel demands all; and, after deducting the necessary expenses of my

family, I intend to give God the rest." Well, these intentions are
good, but many who plead them may be robbing God. Amid the
multiplying wants of our times, is there not danger in these cases
that, unconsciously, God will be cheated out of his rightful dues,
and get a mere pittance? Have we not reason to think that the
only way to secure him against this wrong is to bestow upon him
the *first*-fruits of our substance?

We follow strict rules in the observance of the Sabbath, giving
to God a definite portion of time. Why not apply the same rule
to our means? What Christian would say, "I will not be bound
by any rule as to holy time; but, when I have taken what I need
for myself and family, God shall have the rest"? Amid the multiplying demands upon our time, who would trust himself?

Again, it is said, "It is too much trouble to keep this bank-
account with God." Yes, to him who has no heart in the service
of God, it may seem trouble; but to those with whom religion is
a life, a daily walk with God, this recognition of stewardship will
be a constant source of delight. Prayer without ceasing is trouble
to him who has no heart in it, daily watchfulness over besetting
sins is trouble; but, to him who makes the service of God more
than meat and drink, these duties become privileges.

Advantages.

1. Nothing else gives so clearly the idea of stewardship as this
daily reckoning with God. Ministers will not waste strength and
patience in continual pumping to keep the channels of liberality
full, but the streams of charity will flow from an interior river of
living water. Our giving will not depend upon the pungency of
sudden appeal, or upon the tact and shrewdness of the operator
upon our sensibilities, but upon our well-considered obligations to
God and to the spread of his kingdom. Conscience and principle
will take the place of irregular impulse and fitful sensibility.

2. All the difficulties in the way of weekly offerings will be
obviated. In the portion consecrated to God, every one will have
a gift to bring on each recurring Sabbath. The difficulty of securing a consent of the will to give to the treasury of the Lord what

has been already appropriated to the multifarious uses to which property is now applied is the mountain barrier in the way of systematic giving. Assign unto the Lord *first* the fixed portion which is his due, and all these difficulties vanish.

3. We shall then study with pleasure the great enterprises of the age. It will be a matter of interest to select the channels in which our benefactions may flow, so as best to honor God and bless mankind. The missionary sermon will no longer be regarded a tiresome device to extort our hoarded gains, but a source of coveted knowledge, aiding us to determine where we may send our gifts.

4. We shall thus be enabled to use the world as not abusing it. The thought that all our work and gains are passing in review before God will be a restraint upon those unworthy practices and doubtful methods that now deaden conscience and paralyze the Christian life.

June 1, 1876.

IMPORTANCE OF A HIGH IDEAL TO CHURCHES AND MINISTERS.

We speak of model churches, of what a church ought to be, as if there were no possibility of realizing the conception. This is wrong. The carpenter has his plan for a house, and expects to see it realized in the building. If it is not, his disjointed, unmatched work is a source of annoyance. I read of the sick architect of the bridge across East River, New York. As he was lifted so that his eye caught for the first time a glimpse of the great piers, he said, " It looks just as I expected it would ! " There is something sublime in this realization of an ideal.

The churches would find it easier to keep everything throbbing with life and power than to remain cold and dead. They need a more efficient leadership. God's great care in the promotion of his kingdom has been in the selection of leaders. We must have able ministers or none. Some have entered the ministry who go

to and fro each season, like our migratory birds from Missouri to Minnesota. Unable to manage the smallest churches, they are ready to enter important fields in Iowa, and think themselves competent for any position. When one finds by fair trial that he cannot build up the cause of Christ, why should he not seek another calling?

There is need of pastors who will go from house to house, and kindle in families an enthusiasm for high thoughts and noble deeds. Every home needs a Socrates, to bring in purposes and thoughts different from those that actuate a majority of youth. If the pastor could enter as a friend and counsellor, and direct their reading and plans for life, what a revolution might be effected! I study the power of the old New England pastors in this direction with increasing interest. There is one fact that will remain to the end of time; and this is that the personal, immediate contact of a superior life is the mightiest agency God has appointed for kindling great thoughts and purposes in other minds, especially in youth. I pray for leaders of Israel, like Moses, Joshua, and Paul, to organize victorious churches, to stimulate our youth with a laudable ambition, and diffuse righteousness and truth.

1877.

A NIGHT RIDE.

I took the train to visit our lone Grand River Church, on Rev. David Knowles's field, Saturday afternoon. Reached Winterset at half-past six, and started on foot, expecting to walk about half the way, and go the rest of the distance in the morning. The night was very dark, and the road rough. After going some four miles, I was overtaken by a man in a light, two-horse wagon, whom I hailed and found to be going into the same neighborhood, some fifteen miles from Winterset. He had a lantern, which I held; and we swept on with a will. In going down the bluff to Middle River, the driver's side of the wagon suddenly went down over the

edge of a deep gully, precipitating him head-first into the darkness. The horses did not stop. The wagon dropped on the axle for a moment, when the wheel again struck the bank, and was lifted out without upsetting the wagon. But the shock lifted me bodily, and I followed in the wake of my companion. The sensation experienced, when I saw that I must land it was impossible to guess where, was very peculiar, and not easily forgotten. I have felt the like two or three times before in dangerous emergencies. But, as a kind Providence would have it, I was thrown forward, so as to clear the gully, and alight square on my feet on the solid bank, *lantern in hand.* I threw a momentary glance on my friend, to see whether he was killed or needing immediate succor, and saw him scrambling in the sand below me. All this occupied about a second of time. My whole thought was now turned to the horses. They had never stopped, and were prancing, much excited, down the hill, preparatory to a run. They still kept the road, from which we had varied but two or three feet in going off. Every time I said, " Whoa ! " they would break a little, till a swift run for about forty yards brought me to the bits of the off-horse, which I seized, and we were safe. My friend soon came up, much jarred by the fall, having struck on his head at the bottom of the gully ; but the ground was soft, and the injury slight. He took the lantern, went back, gathered up the cushions, etc., and we went on rejoicing. The Sabbath was a very pleasant one.

February, 1878.

TEMPERANCE REVIVAL.

The Temperance Revival seems to overshadow every other interest just now. It is a marvel. The Red Ribbon and the Blue Ribbon Movement are both operating in various parts of the State. The excitement, the contagion, is wonderful. I think it will operate in favor of earnestness in religion, and be an apology for it among irreligious men, who see how it is with themselves

when aroused to grapple with evil. The movement sweeps like wildfire. The excitement is at its height during the singing and signing the pledge. Knots of men, often of women, form around an intemperate man, and there is no resisting the pressure. Continual cheering is going on from the crowded galleries and every part of the house, as one after another noted " bruiser " goes to the platform to " sign." A beautiful woman stands ready to fasten the ribbon on the dilapidated coat. The only drawback is that the *religious* element does not come in sufficiently. The work has taken hold of the " roughs," and gone down through the lowest stratum. Men from the gutter see themselves the pets of society. The immense halls are crowded almost to suffocation. The odors, sometimes unbearable, tell you the depths have been stirred ; while the coarseness of language and method puts out some of the Christian people, so that they scarcely know what to do. The " roughs," of course, are made prominent, so as to reach their own class ; and the religious element seems almost necessarily kept in the background. I am not criticising the movement, but showing how its force and impetuosity have swept it, to some extent, beyond the reach of our Christian people. But when the excitement has passed, and these newly awakened hopes and aspirations begin to seek their proper objects more calmly, then will be the time for a great religious work, if Christians are only ready.

February, 1878.

IMPORTANCE OF THE THOROUGH CHRISTIANIZATION OF THE UNITED STATES.

It is easier to sweep over wide regions, and partially Christianize them, than to hold them a thorough conquest for Christ. This last work is the crowning test of power.

It was revealed in ancient times that one nation might become the light of the world. What efforts God put forth in Israel for

the salvation of the *home field!* He told his people not to rest until religion was completely established among them; that, if any of the ungodly were left in the land, they would be pricks in their eyes and thorns in their side. The Saviour after his ascension sent especial word to the churches to "strengthen the things that remain."

The Saracens were not the destroyers of Christianity, but God's avenging angels to remove the candlestick when the light had ceased to burn. Turkey and Palestine are hard fields to-day. It is difficult to relight these charred, decaying wicks after centuries of desolation. Austria is a hard field, and Italy and Spain. Must this withering blight ever follow the westward march of empire? Has America no lessons to learn from the voice of God, and the fading glories of a Christian civilization in its ancient seats of power? Must we relinquish our base of operations for the regions beyond? Shall it always be said that Christianity can conquer, but cannot hold the conquered territory? Shall we turn from America to save China and Japan? In centuries to come, shall some Chinaman or Japanese visit the worn-out civilization of America, and attempt to lift it from sottish degradation?

God is speaking to us to-day, by the voices of history, and by his spirit in the hearts of many of his children, to make America *thoroughly Christian* from ocean to ocean. He calls upon us to do this for our own sakes, for the sake of our missionaries in foreign lands, for the sake of the vast multitudes of heathendom, for the sake of the divine glory tarnished by the conquests of Satan on fields once radiant with the presence and power of God. Toward this land, our missionaries from Iowa in Micronesia, Europe, Asia, and Africa, are looking: they plead with us to be true to the trust committed to us as a nation. Brethren on heathen shores, we bid you God-speed in your great and arduous work. With intense interest, we mark your advancing watch-fires; but never for one moment can we admit that you have any more important work or heavier burden than is rolled upon us in saving this land for the central gem in the Saviour's crown.

187?.

By request of the Executive Committee of the
American Home Missionary Society, he made an ex-
ploring tour to Colorado in July and August, 1874,
visiting most of the settlements from Cheyenne and
Laramie on the north to Del Norte and Trinidad on
the south, and traversing extensive regions never before visited by a Congregational minister.   The following extracts are from his report to the society:—

COLORADO: ITS HISTORY.

With deep interest, I traced the history of this remarkable Territory,— its first exploration by the Spanish Captain Corando in
1540; its cession to the United States in 1803, as part of the
Louisiana purchase ; the expedition of Lieutenant Pike in 1806;
of Colonel Long in 1820; of Captain Bonneville in 1832, immor-
talized by Irving in his *Rocky Mountain Travels;* of Colonel
Frémont in 1842; and, lastly, the cry of "gold" in 1858, which
roused a nation's cupidity and covered the plains with caravans of
fortune-seekers.   Colorado was set off from Kansas and a territo-
rial government established in 1861, embracing a region of mountains and plains about twice the size of New England.

Description of Colorado: Its Resources.

The eastern third is an inclined plane, raised by the same mighty
uplift that piled the huge mountain masses.   This comparatively
level surface rises gradually toward the west, and impinges on the
mountain barrier at nearly the same meridian for three hundred
miles across the entire Territory.   On the plains, within twenty
miles of the base of the mountains, along the snow-fed rivers,
and to some extent up the cañons formed by these rivers, have
sprung up the principal towns and settlements ; and here, with the
exception of settlements on the large rivers and a few towns in
the parks, will remain the bulk of the inhabitants.

Agricultural interests are rapidly developing. But a comparatively small portion of Colorado can now be tilled, on account of the scarcity of water for irrigation. Already, on some of the smaller streams, the limit of supply has been reached; but along the larger streams much valuable land remains to be occupied. This limited supply of cultivable land creates a monopoly, which will make horticulture and agriculture exceedingly profitable. The process of irrigation is simple, the soil excellent, the crops large. There are vast parks in the mountains, whose capacity for agriculture has been exaggerated. Their elevation, with the difficulties of irrigation, will prevent extensive cultivation.

Stock-raising has peculiar facilities. In midsummer, the hardy grasses, that more or less thickly cover the plains, dry up, retaining rich juices, the strength of which, from the dry atmosphere and absence of rain, remains through the winter, supplying food for numerous herds. There are at present half a million of cattle in the Territory, with a larger number of sheep, supplying the best of beef and mutton, with wool for manufacture. There is capacity for large increase in this branch of industry, though stock-raising may be limited to the vicinity of rivers, water having thus far been secured with difficulty on the plains. The mountain parks will probably be used for raising large herds to a more limited extent than some suppose, as they would need shelter and hay at times, grass growing too thin for cutting, except on bottom-lands or where irrigated.

Mining will always be an absorbing interest. At first, small towns sprung up as if by magic in the "placer" or "gulch" districts, some of which as speedily vanished, giving many the impression that there is nothing permanent in these mining regions. But gulch-mining has given place in most instances to quartz or lode mining; the lodes of silver and gold growing richer as they descend, giving almost as much permanence to mining as to any other industry. New mines are continually discovered, especially in the San Juan country.

Of coal deposits, seven thousand square miles have been discovered, with an annual yield of two hundred thousand tons.

Some of the finest deposits are in the vicinity of Cañon City, near a mountain of magnetic iron larger than the Iron Mountain of Missouri. Immense iron deposits have been found in other places.

The lumber interests of Colorado need also to be mentioned. Pine, spruce, and fir trees grow abundantly in the mountains; but the central region of the plains, known as "the Divide," is now yielding most of the pine lumber. The product last year was thirty million feet. There are also forty flouring-mills in operation, which last year turned out six hundred thousand sacks of flour, probably unsurpassed in quality by any in the country.

Colorado has attained great notoriety as a resort for invalids, and will be more and more sought after. Pleasure-seekers and lovers of the wonderful in nature will rear splendid mansions in her romantic parks and wild cañons. Cities are rising in various parts of the Territory which compare favorably with those of like size in "the States." It is evident that the present inhabitants have "come to stay," and that Colorado is to develop a sure and healthy growth in population and in all branches of industry. A public school system has been adopted, which is as yet but partially established in the southern counties, controlled as they are by Mexican majorities, which are happily diminishing.

Religious Condition of Colorado.

Congregationalists came to the Territory in perhaps as large numbers as any other denomination; but, with that lack of denominational instincts which has characterized so much of our Western work, entered other communions, and aided in building up other church polities. In 1863, the first Congregational Church was organized at Central City. The following year two more were formed, at Boulder and Denver. We now have eight churches, with two hundred members and five ministers. We find ourselves at this time the smallest of the tribes of Israel. While one or two of our churches are self-sustaining, the rest must depend to a considerable extent upon the Home Missionary Society. Look at some of the causes of this state of things : —

1. Religion from the first has been in a very depressed state in

the Territory. Men came, under a gold excitement, with minds preoccupied. For a time there was no society. There were few families. Men gave loose rein to every worldly passion. Ministers were little cared for. In the hard life-struggle, benevolence, hospitality, and the kindred virtues of the older States, were almost forgotten. This apathy to spiritual things proved depressing to ministers, and it was not hard for them to persuade themselves that they might be more useful in places where larger congregations could be secured with less privations.

2. The denominational spirit has been strong. The great centralized denominations have lavished large sums of money on communities almost indifferent to the gospel. The Episcopalians have some fifteen churches; the Methodists, fifty preaching appointments; the Southern Methodists, some twelve churches; the Presbyterians and Baptists, each about twenty. The Cumberland Presbyterians, the Reformed Episcopalians, and other denominations have several churches. As a result, many small towns have been occupied by various denominations, rallying scarcely a dozen hearers each; while the mass of the people are in the drinking and gambling saloons, or at their business, on the Sabbath as on secular days. It is easy to imagine the effect of this state of things on a New England minister, taught from childhood to cultivate a fraternal spirit toward all denominations. Looking upon these rival interests, he says that he cannot be a party to this denominational struggle, and leaves for some more congenial clime. This is much of the history of the past ten years. Our ministers felt that the field was occupied, and that in withdrawing they solved the problem of duty. Yet it is possible they had not. Congregational ministers who have been long in contact with this knotty problem are inclined to believe that it cannot thus be disposed of. Colorado is peopled with a sagacious, intelligent population, who are not to be brought to the sanctuary and to Christ by mere denominational zeal.

When the "great expectations" awakened in the formation of new towns have subsided, and foreign funds have been withdrawn, and denominational pressure from abroad has somewhat abated,

the people will see their inability to support so many conflicting organizations, and will demand concentration to harmonize these conflicting interests. We have reason to expect that in these new adjustments a portion of these communities will turn toward the Congregational polity.

Moreover, we may hope much from Colorado College, located at Colorado Springs. In the vicinity of this lovely spot is some of the most beautiful, wonderful, and sublime scenery in the Territory. Just beyond Fountain River lie Manitou and the " Garden of the Gods," with the vast mountain range close at hand, culminating in Pike's Peak, whose summit is but fifteen miles away. Here will be the metropolis of the cultured and refined who visit this land. The town is being built under the auspices of a company, who are liberal in their plans for the future. They have given twenty acres in the northern portion of the city for the site of the college.

I have thus attempted to give a brief sketch of Colorado and its demands upon us. Our record has been one of humiliation thus far; but it is not too late to retrieve our fortunes, and not encroach on any other denomination. I need not speak of the sacrifices to be made. In that gospel which has raised up so many in great exigencies to face dangers and endure hardships, there is still ample power to equip men for glorious conquests. Never did I have my spirit so deeply stirred as in some of the remote mining towns in the southern portion of the Territory. Licentiousness, drunkenness, heaven-defying wickedness, are on every hand, with no Sabbath and no sanctuary. It is here that ministers and their families are needed, not to *find* good society, but to *make* it; willing, like the Saviour, to throw their lives into this dark current, that they may purify it. Some tell us that the culture and refinement of Yale and Andover unfit men for this work; but no man can have too much culture or refinement for even these semi-barbaric regions.

In this tour, he found his funds exhausted at Trinidad, an expected remittance not reaching him. In his

Sunday morning walk, while reflecting upon the emergency and what he should do, lo ! something upon the ground attracted his attention,—a roll of greenbacks, amounting to sixty-five dollars. He reported the fact, advertised it in church and newspaper ; but no claimant ever appeared.

In view of the importance of Colorado and the difficulties of that field, the Missionary Society, upon his return from this visitation, desired to transfer him thither ; but Iowa was too dear to him, and his convictions that his duty was there were too strong for a change to be made. He wrote, October 19, 1874 : —

The first effect of your letters was a real womanly crying-spell. You cannot realize how dear to me Iowa has become. Here is the grave of my wife; here are my two children; here are the churches for which I have labored and prayed; here are my helpers with their families at Des Moines (I doubt whether any one else would be willing or able to aid them as I have, or to work successfully with them); here are the weak churches without pastors who look to my visitations, and the churches I have aided in organizing; here is a State capable of sustaining a vast population, that I long to help in lifting into a life of sacrifice for Christ. Everything seems in working order. The pastors are in hearty co-operation with me, and welcome me to all their associations as one of their number. My helpers are out on the field hard at work. All this I am asked to leave, for a field that offers nothing but continual hardships, and that will be occupied by a sparse, scattered, and, I might say in the language of Scripture, "peeled " people. I have seen enough of the Rocky Mountain region to know that there will be continual disappointment to many of the settlers. Its high and arid plains are the home of the locust-plague. Its rivers disappoint by the very limited supply of water.

Its climate is depressing and debilitating to many. As to the churches, there will be no sudden development. It would be folly to press into towns full of strong churches.

And yet, with all this, there is work to be done there; and, if we have any part in this inheritance, it is time we were up and doing. I have heard many voices urging me to go; but one more, the Divine, is needed. My soul has been going up in earnest petition to the great Head of the Church. He must tell me plainly before I can leave a field which I had promised myself I could live and die in.

November 4, 1874.— I have wrestled in prayer over the problem of changing my field of labor, and the thought that there might be greater sacrifice in going to Colorado and that Christ might be more honored had a kind of fascination for me; but, the more I have studied and examined, the more am I convinced that my most important work in Iowa is not yet done. Every one with whom I have conversed felt that it would be a sad waste for me to leave this field. I have tried to impress upon ministers the importance of remaining where they have gained position and influence. I have told the churches, when speaking of my remaining unmarried, that I was wedded to Southern Iowa. I see every year new methods by which more can be accomplished. There is danger that Iowa will become selfish, worldly, luxurious, and expend her wealth in pride and vanity. I cannot then see it my duty to go to Colorado. I believe I can do more for Christ and the souls of men by remaining where I am.

Four years later, early in 1878, the Missionary Society, with a view of enlarging its work in the "New West," determined to reduce its expenditures in Iowa, and asked Mr. Pickett to take the superintendence of the mountain department. He wrote : —

The proposition was first received with great revulsion of feeling, as my attachment to the Iowa churches had become so strong, and Providence had thrown open such a wide field of use-

fulness, that I had come to feel that I wished to live and die on this field. When entering the State, I have often fallen upon my knees to pray for it. Many hours have I spent alone in the wild forests on the banks of the Missouri, looking eastward, and pray- ing for Iowa. It seemed to me that God was saying, " Unto thee have I given this land." I have attempted to secure ministers who would give their lives to Iowa. I have told them I cannot see how men can change from State to State. I have attempted to impress upon new-comers the power of an established reputa- tion, and advised them to lay broad plans to secure it. I have said that with such a reputation no man can afford to change his location. I have spent this year in study and plans of labor for years to come. Now you ask me to leave. I have no home tie to hold me, only an office. But what of the little churches, many of them pastorless, to which I have said, I will care for you,— and the colleges I had expected to help? I cannot yet gain the con- sent of my mind that my sphere is not here; but a shadow begins to fall between me and this cherished field.

A little later, while with his sons at St. Louis, visit- ing his mother and sister, on his way to the National Sunday School Convention at Atlanta, to which he had been appointed a delegate by the Sunday School Con- vention of Iowa, a request came from the officers of the Home Missionary Society that he would proceed at once to Colorado. The necessity was now upon him for an immediate decision. " This letter," he said to his brother-in-law, in whose office he received it, "may change my whole life plans." To the inquiry what he would do, he answered : " I cannot say yet. I do not see my way clear. I will go to the house, and think further about it. I must ask God to guide me. I shall do what he directs." He went to the house, told

his mother, and in a retired room spent an hour in thought and prayer, with a map of the West spread out before him. Coming out, his eye bright and his face lighted with a smile, he said: "It is settled. I go to Colorado. My trip to Atlanta must be given up. I shall return to Des Moines at once, and prepare for removal." His diary contains the following record:—

April 13, 1878, *St. Louis.*— With strong crying and tears, in view of time and eternity, with God as my helper, have decided to enter upon the Superintendency of the Rocky Mountain Department of Home Missions. God has promised to go up with me. I have invoked the Spirit which guided Paul to guide me.

From that hour, he did not hesitate, but prepared at once for his new work. He was married at Wilton, Iowa, April 18, 1878, to Mrs. Sybil B. Rider. They had long shared each other's confidence and esteem, and he was happy and blest in his new home. In a farewell to his brethren, he said:—

I leave not a single enemy. From first to last, I have had the hearty co-operation of every minister. I want to tell them how much their sympathy has helped and cheered me, and how much their forbearance, where there were doubtless many mistakes, has lightened the load of arduous labor. Nine years of close alliance with some of the best Christian workers have made impressions never to be effaced. These have been years of great prosperity, and our relative gain in the State has been greater than that of any other denomination.

There are eight words I hope to bear with me as a talisman in scaling mountains and roaming the trackless deserts:—

"Who loved me, and gave himself for me."

With these words, I hope to be able to say with Augustine:—

"Grant what thou askest, then ask what thou wilt."
"Da quod jubes, et jube quod vis."

With a farewell whose echo will long sound in my heart, I leave you for that vast and needy region, whose mountains of gold and silver can never satisfy the wants of the human soul. I ask your prayers that Christ may be so presented as to raise up many churches, which shall be worthy successors of those among the hills of New England, which have wrought so mightily for freedom and righteousness in this land. It will not be an irksome duty to remember you in prayer, that God may enable you to lay foundations here for great conquests for Christ in the ages to come.

At the annual meeting of the Iowa Home Missionary Society, held at Tabor, May 31, 1878, his brethren recorded their sense of his devoted and self-denying labors in Iowa, his warm-hearted sympathy and brotherly helpfulness to the cause of Christ at large, and their prayers that the Lord would use his experience, power, and practical energy for great results in his new field. The loss of Southern Iowa, they said, is the gain of Colorado.

We are indebted to his pastor at Des Moines for the following account of his life there : —

Coming to Des Moines in the fall of 1871, I met Brother Pickett. It was the first of our real acquaintance, though we had met as students at Andover. Not having been classmates, however, we had barely known each other. But the fact that we had been at the same school at the same time tended to bring us at once together. Our fellowship was cordial and unbroken.

He was a man easy to know, always approachable, with a warm and living interest in the local pastoral work as well as in his own extended field.

To one observing him from the outside, his Des Moines life must have given the impression of a loneliness which called

for profound sympathy. For himself, as fully as any man I ever knew, he could adopt the words of Jesus: "I am not alone, for the Father is with me."

He was no recluse, but he was peculiarly by himself. The two boys, so cherished in his paternal heart, were at Mount Pleasant; and he had nothing that answered to the home life of those happy years when his care was for one limited field. In Des Moines, Southern Iowa was his parish, and one place in it almost as much his home as another.

It was not his habit to thrust himself upon others for society. He rested himself by solitary rambles in the woods and along the river. There was to him a joy and sympathy in nature. He was among the first to know that the wild flowers had opened, and to welcome their coming. He knew the quiet nooks where beauty was fairest, and the points where the landscape broadened out into varied and inspiring views. It was this face to face communion with God in nature that helped him to endure so well the strain his work imposed.

There were homes in the city where he was always welcome, and where now and then he gave himself the pleasure of a social hour. But he was little given to the quest of enjoyment, as such. His time was occupied to the full. His correspondence, accumulating during his absences, his reports to the parent society, which he prepared with much care, and his sermons, addresses, and articles, gave him unremitting employment through more hours of labor than most of his ministerial brethren know. Late into the nights, his lighted window told the story of the busy, prayerful man working within. His meals were often taken irregularly, according to the exigencies of his work. Matters, which perhaps might have been adjusted by correspondence, received his personal attention. Often he would not wait to write letters and look for answers, but, binding on his sandals, would go to see with his own eyes, and help with his presence and voice and purse. So he was always going,— out on the night trains, on the slow-moving freight-cars, in farmers' wagons, in any way by which he could make a point directly, with the least consideration for himself.

When in town, he was careful to attend the social meetings of Plymouth Church, and was an earnest but unobtrusive helper. No soul was more susceptible to gracious currents of spiritual influence, no eye keener to detect signs of declension or advance. None who used to hear his voice will soon forget his deep and tender solicitude for the kingdom of the Master, and for personal anointing.

One of his loving, enthusiastic labors was his paper, — that annual visitor to the churches, so well remembered and so highly prized. To the churches of his superintendence, it was a messenger of cheer, a manual of direction, a chapter of encouragement and inspiration. To the self-sustaining churches, it was a rallying call. To our kindred in the faith throughout the land, it was a cry out of the Macedonia of the West for that sympathy and co-operation by which we must become "one army of the living God." Though emanating from a home missionary superintendent, it took in the whole field of Christian work. He would allow no church to which he ministered in the name of the Home Missionary Society to be satisfied always to receive, or to curtail enterprise under the narrow plea that "charity begins at home." He cared assiduously for this especial field, but never conceived of it as more than a part of that greater field, the world. No man was more alive to the interests of the American Board or the American Missionary Association, though the home field assumed larger proportions with him than with some specialists in religious enterprises.

He enjoyed the happiness of children, and the cheer of playful, musical family circles. In summer, he gave himself a little season of relief. Then his boys were with him. He interested himself in discriminating ways for their improvement, stimulating them in habits of observation and in healthful exercise. They shared his walks in the woods. He owned a boat, which often carried upon the river a joyous load of children besides his own. He unbent himself gracefully to invigorating boyish sports, carrying into them the eagerness and fire that marked his professional toil. He strove to cultivate in his boys a spirit of Christian manliness,

and to possess their minds with a pure and noble ideal of life. They accompanied him in journeys to his birthplace, to the Centennial Exposition, to scenes of natural beauty and places of historic interest, in which one aim prevailed,— to educate them to self-reliance and worthy living.

So the years ran on, until he was taken up from Iowa, where he had become so firmly rooted, and planted in the remoter West. Full of enthusiasm for his new work and of joy in the thought of a reconstructed home, he took his leave of us. It was an inspiration to meet him then, and to feel that we were giving such an experienced, devoted worker to the regions beyond. To us in Des Moines, it was a personal loss. We knew there went from us a man consecrated in every power and purpose to the work of Christ. The fragrance of his life is with us, and the dear remembrance of his name.

A. L. Frisbie.

CHAPTER IV.

SUPERINTENDENT AND GENERAL MISSIONARY IN THE ROCKY MOUNTAINS.

MR. PICKETT entered his field at Cheyenne, Wyoming Territory, May 1, 1878. He met a cordial reception from the members of the Colorado Association, then in session at that place, and won their confidence and love. He established his home at Colorado Springs, and proceeded to his work. He first gave himself to the San Juan region, afterwards to the Black Hills in Dakota, and finally to Leadville. His reports and letters give a graphic view of his labors.

A SABBATH IN SOUTH PUEBLO.

In my first missionary trip, I visited South Pueblo. The *mesa* on which the town is built has much improved since my visit four years ago. The trees, then recently planted along the irrigating ditches, have grown rapidly, and, with the lawns of clover and blue-grass, look exceedingly homelike. The two houses of worship, Northern and Southern Methodist, are still uncompleted, as in 1874. I found there was no regular preaching of any kind. I visited from house to house on Saturday evening, inviting to the Sabbath service, continuing my calls till after dark. At one house, I found, to my surprise, an old Iowa friend, who received me with great cordiality.

The Sabbath dawned without a cloud, with an atmosphere of delicious freshness. With Bible in hand, I walked out on the *mesa* for preparation for the services of the day. Standing on a gentle elevation, I looked westward upon a scene of surpassing beauty and grandeur. Pueblo stands at the base of a vast amphi-theatre. To the north is Pike's Peak, standing usher at the gate-way of the mountains, looking over the plains. With a gradual curve to the south-west, the mountains sweep around Cañon City, and merge into the Greenhorn Range. Still further stretch away the castellated peaks of the Sangre de Christo; while to the south, covered with snow far down their sides, rise the twin summits of the Spanish Peaks, blazing like diamonds in the southern sky. Most fittingly, my Bible opened to the 89th Psalm, verses 11, 12, 13, and to the 90th Psalm. Grander than Tabor and Hermon will this region be, if God will write his name upon it.

The morning was a fitting preparation for the labors of the day. A large congregation welcomed me at the Southern Methodist church, entering with zest into the services. In the evening, a still larger congregation filled the church. With many kind expressions at the close of service, I was invited to repeat my visit. While passing from the church, a woman accosted me with the question, "Why did you not take a collection with such an audience?" and shook hands. As she withdrew her hand, I felt something in my palm, which I found on coming to the light was a dollar bill, which I enclose as the first-fruits unto God from my new field. May it be an earnest of those fruits which shall shake like Lebanon in years to come!

May 26, 1878.

On the last day of May, he started on a tour of exploration, going over the Denver and Rio Grande Railroad, through the Veta Pass, at a higher elevation than any other railroad had then attained in North America, to San Luis Park. At Garland City, he pur-chased a pony for forty-seven dollars and a half, and

rode to Alamosa on the Rio Grande, and to the romantic Mexican town of Conejos, at the southern
extremity of the Park. From this point, he passed
two hundred miles westward, through a continuous
mountain range, to Animas City in South-western Colorado. He then went through the wild gorge of the
Animas, a distance of some fifty miles, to Silverton, the
county seat of San Juan County, where he spent four
weeks in hard missionary labor. Returning by a northern route over the mountains, the trail being then open,
he reached Colorado Springs July 12.

Alamosa, June 3, 1878.— My thirty-five miles' ride through San
Luis Park was a hard one. The wind blew wildly all day right in
my face. I reached the left bank of the Rio Grande as the sun
was setting behind the Sierra Madre, or Mother Range, as the
great central range is called. All day Mount Blanco and the
Sangre de Christo Mountains rose before me at my right, through
which I passed on the cars the day before. I crossed on the
ferry to the town, which has sprung up almost in a night, and has
about eighty rough-looking houses and saloons, with twelve families and two hundred inhabitants, wholly given to idolatry. It is
7 A.M. I start in a few minutes for Conejos.

12 *M.*— I am still in San Luis Park, going south over a level
plain. Not a house since I left Alamosa. Mountains fill the hori-
zon on every side. Grateful, fleecy clouds come between me and
the sun. Mount Blanco's head is covered with cloud upon cloud,
like steps up to heaven. To the south is Round Mountain, toward
which Conejos is in a direct line.

June 4.— My little pony took me safely across Conejos River
last evening. Leaving Conejos at 9 A.M., and passing up on the
banks of the river about eight miles, I began to ascend the mountains. The trees are yellow pine and aspen, mostly. Flowers are
in bloom and strawberries in blossom. The weather is cold, with

snow for two hours, but not remaining on the ground. I met a drove of sheep,— many thousands,— with lambs and some goats, driven by three Spaniards,— a beautiful sight.

6 *P.M.*— The roads are fearfully slippery, mountains precipitous. Three miles back, I struck a fresh wagon-track on the snow, two wagons with three yoke of oxen each, and drivers by their side. They have two or three tons to a wagon. In places, they put on the six teams to pull one wagon up. I told them I must camp with them. We came to a cabin with a large stone chimney. I borrowed matches, and have a rousing fire.

June 5.— The morning has broken clear and beautiful; no wind, and but little snow. I slept on the ground, with an ox-yoke for my pillow. The freighters gave me two blankets. I rose at eleven, when I could not sleep for the cold, gathered together the few coals, and started a good fire. I warmed till twelve; then slept two hours more, when I chopped more wood, built another fire, and slept two hours more. It is now past five. The freighters have not stirred all night. A beautiful creek murmurs near by, which has a deep, wild cañon. The robins! their voices echo from every mountain side. I think the musicians among them have made up a mountain party.

Last night, the freighters baked good bread in a large kettle, fried ham in a skillet, made nice tea, and had syrup. They understand their business. I must now tell them I have the teakettle on, and the fire is ready for cooking. An old magpie is walking in front of the tent, within a few feet of me, trying to steal something.

9 *A.M.*— I am sitting on a mass of winter snow, under a clump of pines in rich foliage. The robins are warbling, the cowslips in full bloom; no sand, but luxuriant soil. I started a little before seven, passing up this lovely cañon, five hundred feet above the river, with thousands of feet still above me. Such fantastic rocks, — likenesses of walruses, elephants, grizzlies, and a perfect bust of Socrates! And such grass! Look at pony, how he feasts beside the cowslips! And the fragrance of the mountain air! Perhaps

there will be a railroad here before ten years, and then the world will see its beauty and grandeur.

9.30 *A.M.*— I am now on the centre of the vertebra of the continent. At my feet, the waters flow east and west. For the first time, the vast western world breaks upon me, as to Balboa.

1 *P.M.*— Descending the precipitous banks of the Chama, I have left the regions of early spring. Here the woods are in full leaf. Some of the way, the valley is a mile or two wide, and fringed with trees far up the mountain. The waters are roaring and dashing, just as they " come down at Lodore." In all my enjoyment of natural scenery, I never had so much crowded into one day. If the seasons were two months longer, and a little warmer, this would be a garden spot. The soil is unsurpassed, very different from the barren sands of San Luis Park. Here are little cherry-trees full of blossom-buds.

I overtook a man half a mile back, and asked if he had anything to eat. He was dressing a sheep. He said he would camp half a mile ahead, and give me some dinner. He has come up with his two boys, and herd of horses and cattle. He is to take the "cut off" to Pagosa Springs. So I will keep with him, as he has a tent and covered wagon.

June 6.— A pot-pie for supper, and another good meal this morning! We reached the "cut off" last night; but a flock of sheep had crossed and recrossed there, so that it was impossible to find a road.

I left my friends before seven o'clock this morning, and, after wandering more than an hour, crossed the boiling waters of the Chama, and at last struck the dimmest road imaginable. I saw a Mexican herding sheep, who motioned to me from the hillside where he had his flock. I waited for him to come up. He bowed, and we shook hands. I could not understand a word but " tobacco." I shook my head, and showed my teeth, to let him see I did not use it.

At 4 P.M., I stopped to bait pony. I tried to eat, but was not hungry. I pressed on, and at length my heart leaped at the sight

of two freighters' wagons coming down into the valley. They said I had saved thirty miles by this "cut off." They had bought a sheep of a Mexican for three plugs of tobacco, costing twenty-five cents. We camped at the first water, built a great fire, and had a good supper.

June 7.—I left my kind friends before eight o'clock, passed down, down, and over another swiftly flowing river, and at 3 P.M. reached Pagosa Springs. Here is a good bridge over the San Juan. There are no high mountains in the vicinity, but the bluffs are about a mile apart. I strolled up the east side of the river a mile to the springs. In the distance, I saw what seemed a log heap burning, from the smoke ; and, walking on, heard the rustling, gurgling sound of the vast cauldron. Imagine a nearly circular body of water, about forty feet across, boiling up a steel blue through the centre and around the edge. You can look down some twenty feet in the centre. A film seems formed, but the waters are perfectly pure, with a strong odor of sulphur and soda. No one dares to get into the central chasm. The water would blister, or boil an egg. But about the edge there are sink-holes, three or four feet deep, in which you may let the water, so as to have it cooler. For a space of forty rods square, the rocks seem perforated with holes, through which the waters flow in all directions. A small brook pours into the San Juan from a dozen channels. Puffs of steam rise over almost all the ground. What a sanitarium! It would bathe the nation, if all the water was utilized.

Here come two Utes, with bows and arrows, to see me write. They bathe with their pappooses nearly all the time.

June 8.—I rose early, and walked along the beautiful banks of the river. The tents of the Ute Indians were stretched along the bluffs on the opposite side of the river, looking very romantic, their ponies feeding, and their flocks of sheep and goats near by. The springs sent up a dense steam in the cool morning air. The Warm Springs in North Carolina do not compare with these. The government retains the ownership, one mile square. There

are no accommodations whatever.   I had a charming bath, though
my pit-hole was most too hot.

I had a nice breakfast,—ham and eggs, goat's milk, furnished
by the Indians.   These mountaineers will not take a cent for anything.   When I went to catch my pony, I saw a man fishing.   He
drew out the largest mountain trout I ever saw, a speckled beauty,
of over two pounds, that made my mouth water.

Now I am in another of the smiling valleys, sweet as the fields
of Paradise, a green lawn, uncropt, bordered with hills covered
with yellow pines, and above all the deep blue sky, with great
white rolling clouds.   Pony walks about, monarch of all this
wealth of grass.   I laugh, when I think that at first I dared not
let go his rope, for fear he would run away. . . . Had dinner with
some freighters, of mutton and warm bread.   At six, reached the
Rio Piedra, a lovely stream, breaking through the wild mountains.
I crossed the bridge, and rode up to a log cabin, without floor,
window, or door ; and here was a woman, the first I had seen since
leaving Conejos, save the Ute squaws.   Her husband has taken
a claim of one hundred and sixty acres, reaching to the Ute reservation south of us.   He has planted wheat, oats, potatoes, and has
some stock.   They are Danes, have a Danish Bible.

June 9.— I sit by this sparkling river, and, under the grand old
pine-trees, amid the awful grandeur of the mountains, which shut
in this valley,— not more than forty rods wide,— have a precious
Sabbath of meditation and rest.

June 10.— I left the quiet home of Mr. Peterson this morning.
My ride has been up and down the mountains all the way.   I have
stopped in a park, surrounded with large pines, under one of which
I am resting, while pony takes to the luxuriant grass.   The robins
are warbling, as usual.   The Rocky Mountains are a vast home for
this most delightful of American birds.   I reach the Pinas River
to-day, and to-morrow Las Animas.

June 11.— I went to Animas,— a town of some fifty raw-looking
houses,— hoping to organize a church ; but, finding the field occu-

pied by a Presbyterian minister, I bade him God-speed, and left immediately. Learning also that Lake City and Ouray were supplied, which I had in mind, I shall not go there.

June 12.— I stopped for dinner with some freighters, to whom I had shown a kindness. They had a loaded wagon and a span of mules. One man stood with the lines and whip, and the other with a club. They ran the mules half-way up the hill, pounding every step. Then the mules would stop, and the wagon would run back to the foot of the hill. This they tried over several times, till the mules were discouraged. I was a-little provoked, and said, "You are not working it right, pushing the mules so rapidly. Take it more slowly." But the driver said, " You must rush them, or they will not go at all." Now I said, "You drive, and we will push." We got half-way up. The mules stopped. I clapped a great stone under the hind wheel, and held the wagon. The mules rested a few moments, and then took the load to the top.

I spent the night with Lewis Carson. He has a nice little farm in the valley, keeps fifteen cows, sells his butter at fifty cents a pound. All kinds of vegetables find a ready market in the mining camps. A short time since, Mr. Carson killed a black bear. A neighbor's boy reported an old bear, with two cubs, on the mountain-side. He took his rifle, went up within shooting range, and put a ball right through it. The old bear did not die immediately, but stood upon its hind legs, walking around to see what could be seen, and looked wicked. The bear started after Mr. Carson. The dog pitched in. The bear started to run, and went nearly to the top of a large pine-tree. It then sickened, and soon fell off. I saw the skin : it was beautiful. The hunters did not dare to look to the cubs while the old one was living, so these beauties got away.

June 13.— Alone in a quiet little park on the Animas, fifteen miles from Silverton. Around me are the lofty summits, covered with perpetual snow, white and pure. The music of the dashing,

thundering Animas fills the valley. This morning has revealed the most wild and rugged scenery I 'have yet witnessed, but not the most beautiful. The Needle Mountain, a sharp peak of solid rock, too sharp for snow to rest on near the summit, is right before me, well known for its choice silver. How grandly the great clouds roll above it in this wonderful azure!

Silverton, June 14.— Here at last! After writing yesterday, I moved slowly on. Eight miles from town, the wagon-road stopped. Then came such a trail,— rocks, rocks! Sometimes I clung to the mountain-side, fearful pony would make a misstep, and go to the bottom. Do not fear for me. I walk in such places. I reached here at 8.30 P.M., having been on the road since before seven in the morning,— so long coming twenty-eight and a half miles. The fading light of lingering day was silvering the snow upon the mountains, the stars were shining, and the moon pouring a flood of light into the valley, as I entered the town.

At the hotel, the landlord said he would take my horse to a stable. I said I would go along, and found there was not a morsel of hay in town. Fed him four quarts of corn, and turned him out on the commons, which are very poor picking. I brought him in this morning, gave him another four quarts, and turned him out again. Only a dollar and a half for a peck of corn!

The field seems open. There is no religious organization or Sunday-school. The town is on the banks of this remarkable Animas River, has two hundred buildings of rough boards and logs. One or two fronts are painted. Mines are in every direction on the mountain-sides. Snow in the ravines comes clear down to the level space on which the town is located.

June 16.— It was snowing hard this morning; snow several inches deep. Soon it began to melt; the streets almost impassable. I went out to the suburbs for the key to the school-house. There were no kindlings to build a fire, but got some at a house near by. A dozen were present; three women. We had excellent singing.

In the afternoon, I walked up the mountain-side to a quiet re-

treat beneath some fir-trees, and poured forth my soul in prayer for this city. I recalled one after another of the promises, and my soul was refreshed. I came down, walked through town, stopped where there were crowds in front of several gambling saloons, and asked them to church in the evening. I remembered what a time I had with the lights at Pueblo. So I went to the school-house, built a fire, borrowed the oil-can and shears at my boarding-place, trimmed the lamps, and had all ready for evening. The snow was now gone, and the streets almost dry. I went over a little before eight o'clock. No one there yet; but soon they came pouring in. Benches were extemporized and brought in; but all could not be accommodated. After preaching, I told them of my coming to the State, of my object, of my anxiety for this community, and of a friend who had just finished his studies at Yale Theological Seminary, and who, I thought, would like to give his life to the work of Christ here. I also spoke of the importance of a reading-room. I asked for an expression, a showing of hands, from those who wished me to send for Mr. Roberts; and nearly every one voted for his coming. I appointed a prayer-meeting and a meeting for organizing a Sabbath-school. A church cannot now be organized to advantage. There are a few persons of various denominations. A minister must cement the elements: then they will be ready to organize.

June 17.— I was called to attend the funeral of a professional gambler. He was gambling Thursday. The next day he was found in a small stream in the mountains, with severe cuts in his head; the first death by violence in this place. The gamblers bought a coffin for him, and were the pall-bearers. We buried him in a romantic place. The river sparkled by us, and the great mountains seemed to bare their heads over our wayward and sinful race.

June 18.— Come with me in my walk before breakfast up Anvil Mountain. Right back of the house, we are up a hundred feet. It was steep! Stop on this plateau. Look into what was once

Baker's Park, now Silverton, at our feet; and on the other side, half a mile away, the Animas. Beyond rise abruptly the majestic mountains. A little way up is timber line, and then awful ruggedness, snow and rock. How the morning sun pours into this sidehill! Look at the aspens,— see their fresh leaves. In ten minutes, we can walk up to where they are just budding. See the delicate flowers,— here a little fern, and there a strawberry in full bloom; yes, a number of them among these rough rocks. Look at those chipmuks, such as we used to see in childhood in Ohio. How they play amid the rocks! A dozen are in plain sight. And the robins,— we thank God that they are here to make it so homelike. How sweetly they fill this sparkling air with melody! But up we go, and pause beneath the dark pine. Here we stop at this great stone, my altar of prayer. I pray for loved ones, for this city, for the gamblers, for all; then, from these lofty heights, I pray for my field, for Iowa, for our nation and the world, that Christ's kingdom may come. But the great heights still tower far above us, and we must go down.

I went three miles to visit the miners on Hazelton Mountain,— one of the richest silver mines in the vicinity,— passed up the Animas, and took a trail almost to the summit. The first mine I entered was the Aspen. The foreman lit a candle and took me into the shaft, which runs straight into the side of the mountain. We went on and on, many hundred feet, and came to the men, who were following a bright vein of silver-bearing rock, about two inches thick, in the solid granite. They were working, clinging to that little vein. I had a pleasant chat with them. They have no religious privileges. Plans are running through my mind of a reading-room in town, and of gathering papers to send out in packages to the mining camps every week.

June 22.— From my door, looking eastward, the vast Hazelton Mountain rises before me, covered with snow, with a strip of deep blue sky; above, a pure white cloud stands out from the deep blue,— and all so near! Each look is an inspiration. You can almost touch these mountains, covered with trees to the timber

line. They are only half a mile away, so that you can see every
limb and leaf almost. The weather is superb. I expected, with
snow on the mountains, and some drifts not yet gone, I should be
very chilly, but not at all. Walked to Pickett's Hill this afternoon,
and studied on my sermons. I saw from the hill the mail coming
on a mule; mail-bags piled high, with the carrier on a horse behind. You would laugh to see these trains of donkeys, now loaded
with dry-goods boxes till you cannot see mule, now a hardware
merchant with stoves, now with ladies' large trunks. The patient
things! We could do little in the mountains without them.

June 23.— Preached, and organized a Sunday-school, and lectured on the two books, Nature and Revelation.

June 27.— Last night I started the fire at the school-house for
prayer-meeting; took over lamps, and, with all comfortable, had
an excellent meeting. Went up Anvil Mountain this morning to
the summit, and had a good wholesome day in the silence of the
fir forest. Read Deuteronomy nearly through amid these scenes of
awful grandeur.

June 29.— A white frost every night; but the weather continues
magnificent. No winds in this quiet retreat, not a particle of dust.
I see a growing interest in spiritual things. Made pleasant calls
all the afternoon, yesterday. Had talks with Catholics and
infidels, and was always treated respectfully. I saw one miner
wipe the tears from his eyes with his great, rough hand, as I talked
with him.

June 30.— The Sabbath dawned beautifully. I built a fire for
church early. We had a house full. At night, I got more seats;
but the crowd pressed in, packing every part of the house.

July 7.— Nearly every child in town in the Sunday-school.
The gamblers of the Jockey Club brought me fifty-three dollars to
purchase a Sunday-school library,— money left from the festivities
of the Fourth.

Mr. Pickett regarded his first efforts in planting religious institutions in his new field with peculiar interest, especially as a test of his cherished plan for uniting persons of different denominations in new towns in one organization. It is obviously impracticable to sustain several denominational organizations in a small town far separated from other communities. Division in such circumstances is weakness and dishonor. By the congregational idea of gathering the whole Christian element in one church, he hoped to solve a difficult problem in the evangelization of our country, and raise up churches to support their own religious institutions. To sustain churches of the various denominations in the smaller towns and mining camps would impose a continual drain upon Eastern churches, and be disastrous to the communities themselves. Hence, he asked Christians of all names in these places to unite on a simple, evangelical basis, upon which all could agree, and to regulate their own affairs, free from extraneous control. He promised them the hearty sympathy and aid of the Congregational Churches of our country, who, he told them, "would rejoice more in seeing these communities walking in the freedom of the gospel than in the possession of all ecclesiastical power over them. We have no peculiar body of men or peculiar form of creed or large establishments of vested interests to tighten the bands of ecclesiastical control, but a form of government, and a simple evangelical faith, which place in one brotherhood all of Christ's followers, leaving great freedom for wide and varied co-operation."

In accordance with the request of the people, he procured ministers for South Pueblo and Silverton, who at once entered upon their work. The Arkansas Valley and the new camp at Leadville now called for his labors, and he wanted to go thither ; but, in view of the great destitution in

THE BLACK HILLS,

he went immediately to a survey of that field. Taking a coach at Cheyenne, on the Union Pacific Railroad, he travelled, almost due north, some three hundred miles, to Deadwood. Two hundred miles of the journey were across vast and romantic plains, with here and there rugged rocks and bluffs worn into fantastic shapes. The last hundred miles are mainly through the Hills, almost to their northern extremity. To the eastward, the plains stretch several hundred miles to the Missouri River, on the north beyond Bismarck, and on the west to the Big Horn Mountains.

From out this vast plain has risen, apparently by a single convulsion of nature, the Black Hills, consisting of igneous and metamorphic rocks, thrown up almost perpendicularly, forming a mineral belt, some twenty miles wide and eighty miles in length, containing deposits of gold and silver. The country consists of a succession of romantic hills and valleys, covered with dense forests of yellow pine, which give the Hills their dark hue and name. In the valleys are deciduous trees,— such as ash, elm, iron-wood, and oak,— and in many places a profusion of flowers. Here were gath-

ered some twenty thousand people, the centre of population being near the northern boundary, in the vicinity
of Deadwood. Here, gulch-mining was begun in 1874;
and a town has risen, full of business enterprise.

From a survey of the field, Mr. Pickett was deeply
impressed with its importance. On his return, being
detained by high water at Jenney's Stockade, July 24,
he devoted the day to prayer for the Hills, when the
work that he was to do there came to his mind in vivid
and distinct outline, so that the accomplishment of it
scarcely made the facts clearer than they then appeared
in vision.

After dark of this day, he took the coach for Cheyenne. He was the only passenger, and rode inside for
the first ten miles, when, weary of the loneliness and
the jolting, he got outside with the driver, who was
glad of company in a region where several robberies
had recently been committed, and who had been driv-
ing a few weeks before, when three men were shot.
They passed that spot at midnight, and soon after
where another driver had been shot the previous season. They came on through "Robbers' Roost," and
were within two miles of the station at "Old Woman's
Fork," when, as the horses were walking up a rather
steep rise, a voice from the left front said, "Hold up
there!" and six masked men sprung up, and levelled
rifles on them. Mr. Pickett immediately said, "Gentlemen, you are in poor luck to-night. Only two on
board,— the driver and a preacher." The response
was, "Get down from there!" As he got down, the

rain which had been collecting on his hat commenced running off. He raised his hands to take off his hat, which they thought a move for his pistols, and pointed their guns on him. He did not pretend to notice them, but gave his hat several vigorous shakes. As he put it on, the leader asked, "How much money have you?" "Three or four dollars," was the reply. "Is that all?" said the leader. "I guess I have about that," answered Mr. Pickett. Seeing the rifles pointed at him, he said that he had no fire-arms, and never carried any, when they pointed away from him. It was now raining harder, and he said, "Driver, it is raining so hard that I will not get on with you, but will get inside, as soon as these gentlemen will let us off." At this, the leader said, "Get in there!" Mr. Pickett thanked him, and entered the coach. The robbers then threw out the mail-bags, and, touching Mr. Pickett's valise, asked pleasantly, "Is this your valise?" "Yes," said he, "valise and blanket." "What have you in it?" "Some clothes, shirts, and a Bible." It was their last word with him; and he sat for half an hour looking on the robbers, as they poured out the contents of the mail-bags. They kept the registered letters, tore open those supposed to have money, put the others back, and handed the bags to him, which he took, and laid down. Then, after breaking open the express-box, they said, "Go on!"

At home for a few days, he enjoyed a view of the total eclipse of the sun in the clear air on July 29, and departed on the 5th of August, to prosecute his mission in the Black Hills.

Aug. 9, 1878.— On we go, night and day; the coach full. I had to sit upright. It made me ache at times. An army officer was with us, going to Fort Laramie. He looked half-drunk, when he got aboard. He drank at every station. After midnight, he was very sick, threw up his hands with a terrific groan, as in a fit. He thought we were attacked by train-robbers. A fat woman in front of him was greatly frightened. We cried to the driver to hold up. We soon dragged the officer out on the ground, that he might lie horizontally. It was some twenty minutes before he " came to." He knew nothing, when we lifted him in. Such national defenders ! . . . For the last thirty miles, we have been among low hills. You never saw flowers so plenty and beautiful, even on the prairies of Iowa.

Jenney's Stockade, Wyoming Territory, August 10. — We reached here at 10 A.M. Our passengers were much excited last night, gave their money and watches to the driver, and all came inside. But it was so crowded I went outside till one o'clock this morning. As the driver said, " This would be a place for the road-agents," as the robbers are called, I thought of the verses : —

> " He shall cover thee with his feathers,
> And under his wings shalt thou trust."

We are all thoroughly tired. The fat lady is smaller.

11 *P.M.*— At Deadwood, after sixty-six hours of terrible jolting.

Lead City, Dakota Territory, August 17.— Off to the hills away, looking down on two cities ! Then, treading the ridge for a quarter of a mile, I came to the highest summit of rocks. Here I sat for an hour, pondering, meditating.

The woodpeckers were crowing in the old dead trees. The little chip-squirrels were lively. Two came up to visit me.

> " They are so unacquainted with man,
> Their tameness 'tis shocking to see."

The little fellows came near, bobbed away again; touched my boot, away again; then up my leg, into my lap, on my Bible, and

commenced nibbling my fingers. At this, I stirred a little. Off
they whirled in a moment.

Near a high ledge, I found a cave, into which I went some forty
feet. It smelled so strong of old Bruin that I felt really ticklish.
There was a nest of leaves, and the unmistakable bear smell. But
no bears are found here now. The smell must have remained for
a year or two.

I saw yesterday a splendid specimen of gold ore in rotten
quartz. It weighed two pounds, and contained about eighty
dollars' worth of gold. The free gold was all through it. I took
a stroll among the mines and mills, and saw the great iron stamps
come down on the ore, and crush it. One mill has eighty of these
stamps. They make a fearful racket.

August 26.— The past week has been one of unremitting but
hopeful labor. I have visited nearly every house and miner's
cabin in the town, and been cordially received. One day I spent
eight hours in steady calling. The work is the greatest I may
ever have in my mountain field. Silverton is completely dwarfed
by it. One week ago last Sabbath, a committee was chosen of
four reliable citizens, formerly members of Baptist, Methodist,
Presbyterian, and Congregational churches, to prepare a Constitution and Articles of Faith, which would be acceptable to all
evangelical believers. They agreed upon articles of faith, and
prepared a Constitution, by which the church is to manage its
own affairs, and at the same time be connected with the Congregational churches of the country, because in so doing it may
maintain its freedom, while joined for aid and sympathy with
a body that is universally known for liberality of Christian sentiment. The Constitution and Articles were adopted with great
harmony. Last evening twenty-one persons united in the organization, and in a crowded house, in the theatre, covenanted with
each other to lift up the standard of the cross in this needy city.
Resolutions were passed, requesting me to secure a minister. It
was the first effort here at Christian organization. In fact, I am
the first minister to preach a sermon in this town of two thousand

inhabitants. Nearly one-half of the members are ladies, who will be very helpful.

Sabbath morning I preached at Deadwood to a full house,—a very intelligent audience. The need of a minister there is also imperative. There is no field in our whole country where the demand is so pressing. I wish I had the ear of all our churches, to tell them what a work God is throwing upon us to-day. The Christian element in these mountain towns must be united in churches free from denominational control. This is the special work of the Congregational churches. We can harmonize this element as no other denomination can.

A sorry lot of passengers came in at Deadwood the other night. They were robbed six miles of where we were robbed. There were three robbers. They made seven passengers hold up their hands, which they tied behind them, except the two women, whose stockings they slipped down, and took out money about the ankles. They got a watch and some three hundred dollars. The mail was robbed, not so carefully as the other time, but strewn all about.

I made a number of calls in Deadwood, and found some cultivated, excellent women, with tasteful homes and flowers and mosses. How soon the hand of refinement will deck these wild hills with the evidences of culture !

I visited the Chinese quarter. Went into one of the opium dens, and saw pipes and opium in abundance, and a beautiful little Chinese girl, about three years old, jabbering in Chinese like a race-horse. The Chinamen bought her in San Francisco for one hundred dollars.

The other evening, while sitting on the piazza, enjoying a display of nature's pyrotechnics, a horseman rode up in the drenching rain, and in a strong Irish accent inquired for me, asking several times if I was a Protestant. He wanted me to attend a funeral in Central. A man's wife had died, leaving a babe. He was very poor, he said; but they would take a collection for me. I said, " No, my friend. I will be glad to go for nothing, and help in the house of sorrow." So I went in a drizzling rain. In walking up the gulch to the house, I saw a silver quarter in the

mud. I went into a neighbor's house to see the babe, and presented him with the quarter. The miners were much pleased.

Central, September 2.— Was sick Saturday, and did not go out all day. In the cool of the evening, I walked quietly to Deadwood. As I was leaving, Miss H—— left the crowded table of boarders on whom she was waiting, and slipped a silver dollar into my hand, saying very low, " Do not walk," and glided back to her table. What could be more beautiful than such acts of womanly kindness? They bring tears to my eyes. But I preferred a slow walk, as I had been sitting all day.

At church, the house was full. I invited those who love the Saviour, members of churches, and those who have been from home so long they are not sure of their membership, but feel the love of God in their hearts, to communion. The stillness was remarkable. I was surprised at the number who communed.

September 3.— Went to Spearfish through deeply wooded hills and valleys,— so there is plenty of material for building,— then we suddenly broke out upon the prairies, with green hills in the distance, rounded into varied forms of loveliness and beauty. I was beside myself with delight at this release from the cramped gulches, where I have spent so many weeks. We rode through gently undulating prairies, among farms, with wheat in stack, oats being harvested, fine gardens, and great fields of potatoes. We struck the town of Spearfish, on the beautiful little river of that name, about 6 P.M. I walked over the town, and asked every one to get me out a congregation. The little school-house was full at 7.30 P.M.

In the night, what a change! The wind north-west; foggy, drizzling. I walked to the river which irrigates the valley, and to some large springs, the waters of which flow in a beautiful brook through the town. There are three small stores, two hotels, a saw-mill, and a flouring-mill under way. There are ranches for eight miles to the Sweet Water. Here will be a Sanitarium for the Hills. I told them I would come back, and work over the whole valley. How little I knew, when shrinking from coming, that such wealth of opportunity was before me!

September 17.— A church organized in Central, with twenty-seven members.

September 21.— A pleasant walk of seven miles, and two rides (eight miles) to Spearfish. What quiet and rest in the sweet fields, the gushing springs, and the sparkling river! Half a mile from the road, two men were found hung,— one a butcher from Deadwood, the other lived in Spearfish. I attended the funeral of the latter. They were stealing cattle, and the ranch-men found them. They have no sympathy here. At evening, I started down the valley,— just a garden-spot. When half-way to the Red Water, the project of an academy at Spearfish dawned upon me. It thrilled me, and I had to speak of it. The first man I met said, " Now, I will write to my wife, and she will come on with the children to live here." Every one is charmed. It is the only place for a project of the kind in the Black Hills.

Deadwood, September 26.— Arranged for organizing a Bible Society for the Black Hills.

Spearfish, September 30.— I have gathered together the Christian element, and aided in organizing a church of eleven members. On the Sabbath, we celebrated the Lord's Supper for the first time amid these beautiful surroundings. About seven hundred dollars was subscribed, without any pressure, at the morning meeting, for building a church, increased to-day to one thousand and twenty-five dollars.

I shall never forget my first view of this delightful valley. Rising in the Hills, the Spearfish River flows with great rapidity some ten miles north, till it empties into the Red Water. It forms a valley about two miles wide, easily irrigated, and one of the most productive and romantic, I venture to say, in the world. To the westward extend lofty hills crowned with pine ; while to the east, from out the plain, rises Lookout Mountain, with its slopes covered with rich grasses and flowers. Near where the pure and sparkling waters flow from out the hills, the town is located, containing some two hundred inhabitants, but destined from its

healthfulness and beauty to be a favorite resort for the dwellers in the Hills. I passed down the valley, the first minister who had traversed it, visiting the ranches along its whole extent. Covered with abundance, it seemed a very Eden. Glancing down the future, I saw this luxuriant valley adorned with Christian homes, with school-houses at intervals, and happy children fitting for life's duties. The health and striking beauty of the place, the cheapness of living, the facilities for building, and the opportunity for gathering miners' families to be educated, all impressed me as favorable for planting an institution of learning which should be a permanent blessing to the region.

Deadwood, October 9.—I called to see the assayist at the California Mine. He was running a gold brick. The furnace was white heat. With thick gloves, he opened the door, seized the retort with large tongs, and poured the contents into the mould. The brick was a beauty. I carried it around some time. It was all I wanted to carry. Worth about seven thousand dollars.

The Congregational Association of the Black Hills was organized October 10, embracing the churches of Deadwood, Lead, Central, and Spearfish. Papers of a high order of merit were presented, and the occasion was richly enjoyed. Said one of the delegates, "Is it possible we can have such a gathering as this, where recently was only a howling wilderness?"

On the evening of this day, I learned that a brother from Galena, a mining town some ten miles east from Deadwood, wished to see me. I accompanied him on his return home the next morning, and preached that evening, to a crowded house, in the little school-house. The crowd filled the aisle, and stood so thick about me that I could scarcely make a gesture. I found a number of intelligent families in this silver-mining camp. They were very desirous that I should return and aid in organizing a church. I returned the following week, and aided in uniting in church fellowship seventeen persons. There was no denominational feeling in any direction.

October 17.—I go out of the Hills, from Galena, nearly due north to Crook City, in an opposite direction from the old route.

Mr. A—— walked with me a mile to the top of the hill over-looking the deep gulch of the Bear Butte Creek, in which Galena is situated. We knelt in prayer. I then struck out on quite a good road, Bible and overcoat in hand. The morning sun was glorious, the deep pine woods beautiful. Not a house for eight miles. Now, I walk in the valley, where there are deciduous trees enough to remind me of home, oak-leaves flying about; now, on the ridge of hills, looking off on the plains. Now a chip-squirrel clucking so leisurely, now a red squirrel quacking as if the welfare of the universe depended on his effort. I was saying all the way: "What has God wrought? May I never fail to ascribe all the praise and honor for what has been done in the Black Hills to Him to whom it wholly belongs! May I never forget God's appearance and revelation to me at Jenney's Stockade and in the valley of the Spearfish! O Lord, abide with these churches through many years to come! Go up with them to spiritual conquests, and get to thyself great glory in these Hills."

After walking about ten miles, I came into hills and wide, grassy valleys; and, after four miles more, to Crook, a small, dilapidated town on the Whitewater, which receives the Deadwood Creek, and its thick, stamp-mill stain, red as blood.

Crook City, October 18.— Called all over town. Had crowded services. The whole town seemed to come together, packing the room. There are only a few Christian people here,— not ripe for an organization. I talked freely with several, and was surprised to find their views harmonizing with mine as to the peculiar facilities of Congregationalism to meet the wants of these communities.

Rapid City, October 21.— Rode here, thirty-five miles from Crook, nearly south, on Rapid Creek in the foot-hills. Visited the mining camp at Rockerville, fifteen miles south-west, and preached in Rapid on the Sabbath. This is on the east side of the Hills.

Ten passengers in the coach! Two "road agents" were on, going to Cheyenne for trial, shackled hand and foot. I looked at them, wondering whether they were the same who stopped me. Two guards were along, heavily armed. I had to ride backwards. Was very sick.

6

After an absence of eighty days from home, Mr. Pickett returned to Colorado Springs, October 25, and was employed upon his large correspondence, in endeavoring to procure suitable ministers for the churches he had planted, in plans with reference to other sections of his field, in attendance upon the meeting of the Colorado Association at Greeley, in reading and study, and in preparation for the labors of the winter. He was anxious to enter upon work in needy places that he had not visited. His explorations had but touched the eastern boundary of the Rocky Mountain District. He saw a vast region toward the setting sun to be occupied. He longed to help in promoting education and religion in Utah and New Mexico. But as the wants of the Black Hills were so urgent, and as he could not at once secure laborers for the field, he determined himself to return thither. After a hard and weary journey, he took up his work where he had left it.

Rapid City, Dakota Territory, December 8.— Reached here Saturday, at four o'clock in the morning. Called on a large number of people that day. Preached Sabbath morning and evening. House more than full at night. We talked up the matter of organization. All were pleased. We appointed a committee of three to look to the matter.

Rockerville, December 12.— My room is a large log room, adjoining the hotel, which is also log. Two bunks are fastened up on the west side. The south one is mine. The room is so cold that I do not more than half sleep. Water froze solid. All the houses here are log. I took a daylight walk, to look upon the rising sun. Here we see the magnificent plains, more beautiful than where

I was in summer. No such deep gulleys, prairie and woodland about half and half.

I called on an old lady from Michigan. She looked coldly upon me, as much as to say, "What do you want?" I said, "I am a Congregational minister, calling to see what can be done for the religious welfare of the community." Her face lightened, like the sun breaking out of a cloud. She reached her hand to me, and said how glad she was to see me; that she had written her daughter to-day how much a missionary was needed. I had a very pleasant call. The evidences of refinement were all about,— a pretty ivy, a calla, an oleander. After calling through the west part of the camp, I walked to the woods for prayer and meditation. It is so still here, no wind, the valley full of oak-trees, with pine all about them. Ragged, perpendicular rocks spring up on every side, making the scenery very romantic. I walked away into the deep, solemn quiet of the hills. The ground was richly carpeted with a thick evergreen,— kinnikinnic,— which is smoked by the Indians. God seemed near. I thanked him that I could preach his great and glorious truth. I never felt more like rejoicing in my work.

This is a beautiful and healthy place. The water is excellent. The air coming through the vast pine forests is sweet as the breath of spring. I think the cars will come here some day from Cheyenne, or from another point, in twelve hours. These Hills are too beautiful and too productive not to draw a railroad within a few years.

In calling, I found a number of Catholic families. All treated me kindly. There are some excellent people here. I took dinner with a gentleman who went to the academy with me in Kingsville thirty years ago. His house is on the borders of the vast forest. How romantic the hill and vale, and rugged rocks of granite tilted up perpendicularly! Now and then I climbed to their summits.

Rapid City, December 17.— It was so cold, I determined to walk from Rockerville. I dreaded the prairie road, so, with my love of adventure and romance, struck out on my own hook straight as

a bee-line for Rapid. It was up and down, rocks and hills. Two miles out, I struck a miner's cabin,—an old man all alone. His wife had died. He said I was going in the right direction. He came out, and pointed me on. I crossed Rapid Creek on the ice, and went down its romantic valley, amid glorious scenery, and great meadows with abundant grass uncropped, except where the deer had come out from the deep shadows of the bordering pines to feed. I started up a deer in a ravine, but with a crackle of brush he was away among the low pines. The road crossed the creek several times. I crossed twice on the ice, several times on foot-logs, but once could find neither; had to pull off my boots, and wade. But a cabin was near, and I ran to the fire, and did not take cold. Got here at 6.30 P.M., which all counted good time.

December 19.—A hard day's work at Deadwood, visiting from house to house. Women washing amid frost and cold, looking so feeble; children deformed from vices of parents.

December 21.—Started from Deadwood at 5 A.M. on the coach, snow six inches deep. Had a beautiful ride on the box with the driver. We found no snow after twenty miles. Reached Rapid City at 2 P.M. I visited the school. In the night, the wind blew fearfully. This morning the snow is flying. The people in Deadwood were determined to have me stay another day; but I had work to do here, and I have learned to do things when they ought to be done. If I had stayed, what a time I should have had! I preach here to-morrow, and shall feel no anxiety about the storm. But the roads are full of freighters. What a time they will have with their long teams, sometimes of horses, sometimes oxen, sometimes mules!

December 23.—A new hall is just completed and plastered, a rarity for the Hills. A good lady wanted our meeting held there, as a sort of dedication of it before the dance of Christmas eve. As it was stormy and blowing fiercely, I hesitated, and thought it best to go into the little school-house; but I consented, and went from house to house all over town, telling of the meeting. I longed to impart some spiritual blessing. The people gathered in

good numbers. There was an organ, fine singing, and evergreens for a Christmas tree.

December 24.— Returned to Deadwood, and visited there, and in Central and Lead. We had a Christmas tree at Deadwood. So much travel is attended with considerable exposure. God is so kind, to give me strength for this severe work in this severe weather. Twelve degrees below zero at sunrise Christmas morning. The next morning, finding the thermometer only down to zero, I rode to Rapid, and walked to Haywood and Rockerville, and back to Rapid, holding meetings on successive days in those places.

Spearfish, January 1, 1879.— The coldest day I think I ever experienced. The air cut like a knife. I left Rapid at daylight, rode three hours with the driver, then took the inside. We reached Crook at noon, rode on to the Centennial Prairie. The driver wheeled his six splendid horses out into the snow-drifts, and struck across into my road to Spearfish. Was not that kind? I walked ten miles, got in about 6 P.M. I found the road filled with teams going to a ball, but I preferred walking. The academy has assumed a more tangible shape. Lumber is now on the ground, ready for building when spring opens.

January 3.— Rode to Deadwood, thermometer twenty degrees below zero, and visited in Lead and Central. I have endured for the past few weeks about all that human nature can endure, it seems to me, of hardship. The cold has been so intense as to prostrate one, and almost take the life out of me. It has been rather gloomy work, calling in Central. The homes look so forlorn,— miserable shanties, with no comforts. Disappointments and trials have apparently hardened people, so that their minds seem stupid. Numbers are going to Leadville, Colorado.

We observed the Week of Prayer for three evenings at Lead. One afternoon, I cut up a sheet of paper with Scripture verses on the topic assigned, which was " Special prayer for all in the community who are or have been professors of religion, that they may be fully consecrated to the service of the Lord," and gave one to

each Christian on whom I called. They seemed to appreciate my calls. I got around at seven o'clock, with one text left. I said, "That must be mine." The house was dark, but the teacher had left a good fire, and swept out nicely. I lit a lamp, looked for my verses : —

> "He giveth power to the faint,
> And to them that have no might he increaseth strength.
> Even the youths shall faint and be weary,
> And the young men shall utterly fall :
> But they that wait upon the Lord shall renew their strength ;
> They shall mount up with wings as eagles ;
> They shall run, and not be weary ;
> They shall walk, and not faint."
>
> *Isaiah* xl., 29–31.

One and another came in, bringing their verses. A stranger, not a church-member, came to talk about building a church. He spoke of the crowd that could not be accommodated on Sabbath night. So, after prayers, we went home through the storm, feeling that we had a good meeting.

Galena, January 10.— I enjoyed my walk to this place. The road was not well broken, so that I got pretty tired. I feel perfectly safe, travelling about this winter. Robbers and thieves cannot secrete themselves by the wayside. The snow is two feet deep. It lies on many of the pine branches like great pillows rounded off by the wind. In some quiet places, the limbs of the pine and spruce are bent down, giving that peculiar weird appearance seen in pictures of northern countries in winter. Sometimes, I traversed deep ravines, where the winter sun never shines, and the pines are shaggy with trailing mosses. I reached here a little after noon. Was so tired I did not go out till evening. The little school-house was more than full. A good audience again the next evening, all that could pack into the house. I called during the whole day, and on nearly every person in camp. We have the most liberal Catholics here I have ever met with. Many of them are among my hearers. The thought occurs whether the time is

not at hand when Protestants and Catholics may feel that they have many interests in common.

Rapid City, January 20. — I lectured at Rockerville Friday, on "A True Life," and came here to a lyceum in the evening, that was started from my New Year's sermon. I read Byron's "Waterloo," and was chosen critic, and one of the judges for the discussion. On the Sabbath, a church of fifteen members was organized, embracing the best, and in fact all the Christian element of the place. The day was beautiful, and the hills and plains seemed to smile approvingly upon the first communion in this hopeful town, at the confluence of the Sidney and Port Pierre stage lines. But the work cannot long go forward in the Hills without ministers to take it up. I wait and watch, asking where are the men to push forward the most hopeful enterprise that has been opened for our churches in many years. God has given me good success, and I must not desert the field until men can come. It has taken much time to regain what I lost in leaving for the month I was home. I seem greatly needed now. There was never so much religious feeling in the Hills. But occasional sermons from superintendents and general missionaries cannot do the work that is needed. Permanent and able pastors, such as unfolded the best type of New England character, are wanted. We must expect some denominational competition. But the Congregationalists were the pioneers, and have built on no other man's foundation. To find a new field untouched by the various denominations can scarcely happen again. If our work is pressed with energy and wisdom, the results will be glorious in coming generations.

One never wearies with the beauty of these wonderful Hills. Sometimes, it is true, the storms brewed in the wild cañons of the Yellowstone and the Big Horn Mountains come racing in reckless license over the weird plains, and strike in boisterous fury. The vast forests of sombre pines, caught by the tempests, sigh and moan and toss, as if in throes of agony. But the storm passes, the clear sunlight pours its wealth of comfort and cheer into the mountain valleys, and one thinks it the most lovely spot in the

world. The atmosphere on the eastern slope of the Hills has a softness and purity at times, which is altogether fascinating.

Rapid City lies on the eastern plains, about midway of the Hills, close under their shadow, on the longest stream that flows from them. The valley is broad, beautiful, fertile, easily irrigated, and dotted with ranches. The Sabbath sun broke over the eastern plains in matchless splendor. The long lines of western hills glowed like a vast diamond in its setting of silvery plains. One seemed to hear from the plains and valleys the tramp of the coming generations, and from out the heavens the angels' advent song.

TO HIS MOTHER, ON HIS FORTY-SEVENTH BIRTHDAY.

I have felt this evening, though pressed with work, that I must stop, and write a few words, at least, to the mother who bore me. I cannot say that time flies very rapidly with me. Great changes make such breaks as divide up the years somewhat. For instance, it seems a long time since I was in mother's room, in St. Louis, with Bible and map of the United States spread out before me, as I prayed for direction as to my future life. Nothing has happened to me in many years that seemed so pleasant as being with you at that time. How strangely God led me there with my boys, and what events were to follow! My marriage, our departure West, that long trip through Southern Colorado, the visit to the Black Hills, strange vicissitudes, exposures, and dangers,— how like a dream, and yet how real!

How little I thought, when in the old log school-house studying in Parley's Geography of the Rocky Mountains, that I should cross alone their wild summits, and feel familiar in their solitudes! What a privilege your boy esteems it to plant the precious gospel his father and mother taught him, in these regions! How grand these beginnings! Faith sees a handful of corn on the tops of the mountains shake like Lebanon in the not distant future. I feel well and strong for the work before me, and delight in it more than in anything I could do in all the world. If I had

all the gold and silver in these mountains, it would be nothing to the satisfaction which I receive from going about doing good.

And now I realize that you cannot be spared to your children many years. I want to tell you how I have been sustained by your prayers in my arduous work. Many times in my talks, I have said: " My mother is praying for me every day. Her race is almost run. She has borne the heat and burden of the day: she can do little now but pray for the reapers in the harvest-field." Never forget your boy in toil and temptation. Pray that the Holy Spirit may rest upon me, that God may give me a burning love for the souls of men, and a faith that will overcome the world as I find it here in its intensest forms, that I may have wisdom and foresight in planting churches, and be so guided in everything that at last I may be able to say with Paul, " I have fought a good fight, I have finished my course, I have kept the faith."

Central City, Dakota Territory, January 28, 1879.

February 3.—Preached to a full house in the morning at Rockerville, and in the afternoon at two o'clock started back to Rapid. I took another cross-cut, different from the one I took in December, thinking I could do better; but it was worse, a considerable part of the way perpendicular, over hills and ravines so dark and gloomy. In the deep glens there seems almost an eternal silence, except the moaning of the pines. The sun became obscured, also the moon, so that I was obliged to guide my course by the outlines of the hills. Darkness crept on. I was no longer weary, but hurried on in a half-walk, half-run. Coming to a broad valley, I stopped to listen several times, and at last heard the murmur of the waters of Rapid Creek, which never seemed so grateful. I struck a road leading two miles down its southern bank to Rapid, which I reached at half-past six o'clock. There was a large congregation in the hall. I was soaked through with sweat.

February 27.—The plains are quite full of Indians. They surrounded Rapid. The soldiers from Fort Meade are after them. They are mostly strolling bands, who have run away from Red Cloud Agency, on the Sidney route. They are running off stock,

and are after the freighters. I do not think they are in much of
a killing mood; but I am glad I am not on the way home just now.

Mr. Pickett continued his itinerant labors, encoun-
tering storms and cold, encouraging and strengthening
the little bands of Christians he had brought together,
harmonizing conflicting elements, setting in order the
things that were wanting, lecturing upon education,
temperance, and literary subjects, helping in plans and
subscriptions for church-building, and looking anx-
iously for laborers to come to his relief, until the
middle of March, when he was cheered by the arrival
of helpers for the work at Lead and Central, and for
Rapid City and Rockerville. Meanwhile, other ministers had taken charge at Deadwood and at Spearfish
and Galena.

With a happy heart, he turned his face homeward,
after four months of the severest labor and exposure
of his life. The stage-route of three days and two
nights to Sidney, which once seemed so formidable,
was now a pleasant pastime. He reached the bosom
of his family on the 21st of March. Upon the report
of his labors to the Secretaries of the American
Home Missionary Society, they congratulated him that
he "had been able to present to Christ for his acceptance an Eshcol bunch of churches, big and succulent
and full of seeds for the future," and told him that he
had probably never done more in an equal time, and
would not be likely to do so much again in the same
space, though he should continue many years. In
view, however, of the extent of his general field and

the openings for his labors in many directions, he panted to press into new regions, and sometimes felt that he was confined disproportionately.long in the Black Hills. But he was too near his work to see it in full perspective and in all its importance.

On his route home, he fell in with the swelling tides of a new migration to the mountains. The roads were thronged with people. The opening of the new carbonate fields of Western Colorado had kindled an enthusiasm scarcely paralleled in the country. Multitudes thrown out of employment in the general business depression of the previous year were pressing into the cañons and valleys and parks of that region. Denver and Colorado Springs were full of strangers. Pike's Peak looked down upon an almost endless procession of wagons through the Ute Pass into South Park and the mountains beyond. Passing south to the line of the Atchison, Topeka, and Santa Fé railway, he was still more impressed with the extent of this westward movement. Standing in the streets of Cañon City, he looked with astonishment upon the throbbing mass of life that was passing through. Going into the principal saloon, he was surprised at the number of drinking men pressing up to the bar. Profanity and drunkenness seemed to rule the hour. He stood in silent meditation: "Are these men to be the founders of empire? Are they to build up the communities that shall possess these mountains?" He thought, by contrast, of the Pilgrim Fathers, and of the foundations they laid, and of the absence of

religious sentiment in this hegira. A heathen state
of society seemed to threaten, instead of a vigorous
and advanced development of Christianity. Barbarism
was the first danger. The prospect was appalling.
He again quickened his steps to follow the adventurers
with the word of life. He wrote:—

That gospel, which has thus far been the hope of our country,
must follow these settlers into the mountain fastnesses; and when
the day of sober reflection and often of bitter disappointment
comes, as it surely will come to many, the minister of Christ and
the Bible must be near, and these wanderers must hear the
Saviour's words, "I counsel thee to buy of me gold tried in the
fire, that thou mayest be rich." It is one of the sweetest thoughts
in this mountain work that here is to be a grand test of the
gospel's power. If it can overcome here, it can anywhere. It
will overcome here; and Christ will be honored gloriously, when
from these valleys and mountains churches shall rise, and devout
worshippers shall exclaim:—

"As the mountains are round about Jerusalem,
So the Lord is round about his people
From henceforth even for ever."

He was also attracted by wide openings for Christian enterprise in other sections. He longed to have
a hand in imparting spiritual gifts to New Mexico and
Utah, where a more vigorous prosecution of church
and school enterprises is demanded, to deliver the
people of those territories from ignorance and debase-
ment and from corrupt ecclesiastical despotisms; and
also to Montana, which was then receiving a larger
immigration than for several years previously.

On the 13th of April, he organized a church with
sixteen members at Coal Creek, and afterwards made

explorations of new mining camps in Southern Colorado. He then visited some fields which were formerly cultivated by home missionaries, but which had undergone discouragement and neglect. He attended the meeting of the Colorado Association at Boulder, and gave a full report of his labors, and especially of his work in the Black Hills. His report glowed with holy fire. He pictured so vividly the valleys and hillsides where he had prayed and gathered churches that the brethren felt themselves transported in his faith. During the latter half of May, he was again in the Hills, spending a day with each of his seven churches, and attending a meeting of the Black Hills Association. He then hastened back to mingle with the tide of travel that he had seen surging into Western Colorado. His letters of this period afford the following incidents :—

Silver Cliff, Custer County, Colorado, April 15.— The morning ride up the Arkansas was beautiful, the river sparkling, the plum-trees, of which there are a great number, in full blossom. The red-wing blackbird was hovering over his swamp home with no fear of the ague, the lark was singing his sweetest notes, and my own heart was full of praise and thanksgiving.

At the Junction, ten miles from Cañon City, we started up Coal Creek two and a half miles, and reached the town. I went to see the coal-bank whence comes the bright Cañon City coal. It is easily worked from the surface, not by a shaft. The vein is five and a half feet thick, sinks about one foot in twenty, and covers a large space. The old miners think it the most perfect coal they ever worked. We passed into the total darkness, each with his miner's lamp, about half a mile. It was dry the whole distance, and a pleasant place to work. The miners get ninety cents a ton

for delivering it at the dump. They can get out three tons for an ordinary day's work, which is pretty good wages.

I called around among the people. The Welsh have large, well-trained families, and are anxious to have them in church and Sabbath-school. The church was organized Sabbath evening. They are all Welsh, and seemed harmonious. Their minister preaches in Welsh in the morning, and in English in the evening. The Sabbath-school is wholly English.

Monday morning, I rose at five, took breakfast, and started on foot to strike the Cañon City coach, but missed my way, and went up Oak Creek Cañon. By hanging to bushes and jumping from rocks, I got two and a half miles in two hours, with one fall into the creek. At last, I got into the road; and the stage with six horses overtook me.

About two miles after leaving Coal Creek, we found snow, which got deeper and deeper, though thawing fast. The bright sun was trying to the eyes. At the Half-way House, the snow was so deep the coach could not go on. Another gentleman and myself took a light carriage, and we reached Rosita at sunset. It was raw and cold, and the town full of snow, with wild mountain scenery all around. To the west is Wet Mountain Valley; and beyond rise the familiar Sangre de Christo Mountains, not more than twenty miles away.

In the morning, I took the coach for this place. All is rush here. I find a number of members of Congregational churches.

Denver, May 1.—With all my love for Colorado Springs, I have to acknowledge that Denver is beautiful. To decorate needs wealth and taste. Both are here. The atmosphere seems more humid. The yards are lovely, the lawns luxuriant, pear-trees and plum in full bloom, large flowering-almonds, white and red, loaded with blossoms, and building going on in every part of the city.

Sidney, Nebraska, May 13.—I had a day of sweet meditation and divine communion yesterday. The white, fleecy clouds floated peacefully in the clear sky, with the mountains in the background, the shadows marching with light step over the tender grass, no

dust, and Nature in her happiest mood. But Cheyenne was raw and cold, as usual. A pleasant ride from Cheyenne here. Heavy rains have robed the earth in fresh beauty. The thin, shadowy cattle are luxuriating. Poor things, which I saw in the cold and storm of last winter browsing on scraps of bushes and cactus, now have a thousand times more than they can eat. But, if they enjoy contrasts as much as we, it is doubtless all right. The lamp-post is pointed out to me, where a murderer was hung last Sabbath morning.

Deadwood, May 16. — I have never seen the Plains looking more beautiful. These vast meadows seemed changed into a parade-ground. Troops of cloud-shadows marched in rapid succession through the whole day. Here and there, great herds of cattle were feeding on the tender grass, green as a wheat-field of young grain. Meadow-larks sang sweetly, and other birds imparted life and movement to these uninhabited regions. Here and there are masses of rocks, and wild buttes worn in fantastic shapes.

Night came at last. The sun sank to rest, the west glowed, and beautifully tinted the plains. Then the stars, one by one, came out of their hiding-places in the arch of heaven. After daylight was all gone, a bird would break out in a little warble, as if dreaming its low ditty. At midnight, the heavens were grand. The evening star had sunk, burning red, below the Western plains. The Dipper, bottom side up, still mindful of the order of the universe, pointed with unerring finger to the North Star,— these stars, as Emerson says,

> "Envoys of beauty,
> Visiting the universe with admonishing smile."

Then rose the moon in the far east, and the first appearance of day. At 3.10 A.M., the larks were pouring forth their matin-song.

May 19.— A glorious walk to Spearfish through the magnificent forests, starting at five o'clock Monday morning. The weather and climate and scenery are perfectly beautiful.

June 3.— At Denver, at the organization of the Second Church.

Leadville, Colorado, June 20.— After a few days of rest at home, I started for this place, to which I have been so long look-ing. With valise well stored with flannels in one hand, a double blanket, shawl, and overcoat in the other, I left Colorado Springs on the five o'clock evening train for Denver. In four hours, we were there, in time to take the Denver and South Park train for the mountains. The seats are too short for good rest; and I was surprised to find how well I had slept when morning came. I rose soon after day. We were passing through low mountains, and beside the sparkling waters of the Platte, which sweeps grandly through the gorges, unconscious of the humiliation which awaits it as it flattens out amid the sands of Nebraska. What a change! Is this dashing, brilliant stream, tearing over the stones along its narrow bed, the lazy, wide-flowing stream of the Plains? So some stirring, energetic youth move out into the dreary plati-tudes of life, losing their energy and power.

I saw a snow-capped mountain in the south-west, as the rays of the rising sun changed it to burnished gold. Now we began to climb in earnest. The train was heavily loaded. One felt like patting the faithful engine, as it stopped, panting for breath, to gain new strength and work up a full head of steam for the steep-est ascents. The scenery was grand in places; and such wonders of engineering skill! I am prepared to say all things are possible in railroad ascension. Horseshoe Bends are passed one after another, and we looked down upon vast solitudes of pines and firs far below, or up to the snow-clad peaks above us. At length, we reached the summit of oozy land, where the skunk-cabbage grows, as I noticed on my San Juan trip last year. The water now began to flow toward South Park. I frequently left the train to climb a hill and look upon the wild waste of distant mountains, or down into the tops of the thickly growing firs, straight as the bayonets of an army on parade. Now we were pent up between moun-tains; again, in a moment, we had burst through. The prison-doors opened, and South Park lay before us like a vast meadow.

A beautiful stream flowed away in the distance, cattle were feeding quietly nearer by, and yonder are the white tents of the town of Jefferson, like some Arab encampment, ready to fold their wings and fly away as soon as the railroad passes on.

A number of familiar-looking Concord coaches are in waiting. I secured a top seat above the driver; nine dollars for sixty miles; the scenery pleasant, both shawl and blanket in requisition. Once the coach struck a stone and lifted on two wheels, where it balanced a little time. I thought it must go over, but we were saved. We passed on through the Park, which differs from San Luis in having several ranges of hills that we crossed, and many little streams made from the mountain snows. We passed through Fairplay, which has two neat churches that are sufficient for the place; and on, above timber-line, snow all about us, but none in the road. Then we were on the bleak summit, nearly twelve thousand feet high, with tall peaks rising above us. Then we commenced descending toward the Arkansas, and I was pointed to the celebrated Twin Lakes, nestling amid the dark pine forests eight or ten miles away.

Eight miles up the Arkansas, we turn to the east, and begin to see the wonderful town stretched along for three or four miles. It strikes one not unfavorably, does not look so very bleak, is pleasantly located on rolling ground in the valley, with mountains all about it. Evergreens, pine, and fir are on every side, though being rapidly cut off; but the small trees are preserved in the suburbs, making cosey retreats for dwellings, which are rapidly going up. The furnaces are in full blast, and the livid slag is being poured out in molten masses. But how shall I describe the homeless, restless men that throng the streets, surging to and fro as evening comes on? I have never seen anything like it. Silverton or Deadwood cannot compare with the wickedness here: vast saloons and dance-houses on every side; triumphal cars of dissolute women, tier on tier, drawn through the streets, with bands playing, the carnival of hell.

The American Home Missionary Society placed the first missionary of any denomination in this field; but his health failed,

and he was obliged to give up his work. The Union Church he had organized soon fell to pieces. A few gathered for our renewed service on Sunday at the Opera House, who expressed great joy that they were not forgotten. Never was there more urgent work before us. We must have an able, earnest pastor here and a chapel this summer.

Monday, I took a trip over the backbone of the continent to the new camps of Carbonateville and Kokomo. I rode ten miles to Chalk Ranch, up the diminishing Arkansas, the valley full of stunted willows, and started afoot to the summit. The scenery became grand, as we climbed higher and higher. Here were drifts of snow. I lay down on one, and made a snow-ball, of course. Beside the snow were the white flowers, such as I saw a year ago. Fleecy clouds moved through the deep blue sky, stooping here and there to kiss the white foreheads of the circling mountains. Truly, heaven and earth met together, a symbol of the union yet to be consummated between these mountain-dwellers and their heavenly Father. We were now at the head-waters of Ten Mile Creek, which flows into Blue River. The scenery is grand,—no cañon, but a pleasant valley. Three miles down the valley, I came to Carbonateville, where I found a few families, and three miles further to Kokomo. Here are foundations of houses in every direction, so as to pre-empt lots; but things look quiet. There are perhaps five hundred people, with some twenty families. No minister had visited here before. I secured a hall for religious service. It was just built, and without a seat in it. I put up at the post-office a notice of preaching that evening, and visited all over town, inviting the people to the service. They helped in getting seats, table, and lights. We put candles in beer-bottles, standing them on the floor. People crowded in, some one hundred and fifty. One-half of them stood. We sang and prayed. I enjoyed preaching to this hungry people. They were very attentive. No public prayer had ever been heard before in this community, no song of praise, no reading of the Word of God.

After a careful survey of the field at Leadville, and at the request of citizens of the place who had been appointed a building committee for the erection of a Congregational church, Mr. Pickett proceeded to Hartford, Conn., to solicit aid for the enterprise. On his journey, he found time to write:—

June 26.—The last part of the ride through Kansas was beautiful, after the heat and dust of the parched plains. The Cottonwood River is romantic in places. There are large, rich cornfields in which one could hide without stooping. For many miles, we moved along the banks of the Kaw River. The sky resembled the paintings with which Prof. Dana used to illustrate the carboniferous era, the sun attempting to struggle through the sleeping mists. The woods looked tropical; the bushes loaded with clambering vines; the beautiful sumach, the honey-locusts and black walnuts clothed in rich foliage, and wild roses blooming everywhere. Here and there a solitary old stub, such as we used to see in childhood in Ohio, has moved the compassion of an ivy to spread the leaf of charity over its naked deformity. Yonder, in the wide heavens, moves with slow and steady flight a blue crane in quest, like some lone preacher, of better fishing-grounds.

June 27.—We have passed into Indiana. Before crossing the State line, we struck old-fashioned woods; and I feel much at home on a clay soil, with grass abundant. From a large red-clover field, the air comes in sweet at my window. Here are beech and maple, ash and elm; and, on all the new fields, stumps, stumps! How I have pulled them out, played around them, and burned them!

June 28.—Here is Lake Erie, that in childhood filled me with a sense of the Infinite.

June 29.—Central New York is a wonder,— so much beauty of scenery, such homes and fine-looking people. Troy is a delightful city. I have enjoyed its Sabbath quiet and the churches. It is evident that all this is due to the religion of Jesus Christ.

Hartford, Conn., July 4, 1879.— I pray to-day for our wonderful country, that the Lord may preserve and bless it, and develop everywhere such a civilization as I see around me here.

The sudden changes of air and temperature which he encountered, and his fatigue, induced a severe attack of rheumatism at Hartford ; and he felt the incongruity of pleading upon crutches for the Rocky Mountains. But he pursued his mission, and in the course of a few days collected twelve hundred dollars. With pleasant memories of the kindly co-operation of Hartford pastors and people, he hastened back, stopping half a day with his mother at Meadville, Penn., and was at Leadville on the last day of July, securing an eligible location, raising additional means, and stimulating the speedy erection of the church. The work was hard and laborious, and taxed his strength and burdened his spirit heavily. Meanwhile, he made a missionary exploration of new fields in the Gunnison River country, and in the early days of September took a brief rest at home. The latter half of the month, he was again at Leadville, looking to the foundations of the church and gathering building materials. Thence he made a visitation in the Black Hills, to help forward his seven churches, and again returned to Leadville, to push on the work which was giving him so much anxiety.

I took the Cañon City coach at Leadville, August 21, for forty miles down the Arkansas River to Mahonville, a romantic little place, with no material as yet for a church. From there, the ride up the valley of the Cottonwood toward the cañon was very pleasant. The mountains are grand; and it seemed much like going

to Manitou from Colorado Springs. The summits of Yale, Harvard, and Princeton rise on either side of the mighty cleft which forms Cottonwood Pass. After riding about five miles, we came into the precipitous cañon, and right up to Mr. Adams' beautiful sanitarium. The Cottonwood murmurs by. The air seemed balmy; and the nervous excitement of the higher altitudes passed away. The springs are almost burning hot, with soda and various medicinal properties, regarded as an antidote to lead-poisoning and other diseases.

The next morning, I set off on a pony over the mountains. After rapid and laborious climbing, at 2 P.M. I stood on the backbone of the continent. It was grand beyond description. Descending rapidly to the west, I reached Hillerton at 6 P.M., near the headwaters of Willow Creek, which flows into the Gunnison. Here I found a camp of about two hundred miners, with perhaps a dozen families. I left an appointment for the next Wednesday evening, and passed on, spending the following night at the first stopping-place, thirty miles to the west. In attempting to save five miles by a cut-off, I was lost twice in the wildest part of the mountains, and at last led my horse over fallen timber and rocks down the steep mountain-side into Union Park, where I struck the road, having wandered from 8 A.M. to 1 P.M. Passing five miles down Lotus Creek, a wild cañon, I came to Taylor River, really the Gunnison, down which I rode twenty miles, and at 8 P.M. reached Jack's Cabin, a weary man.

On the morning of the 24th, I rode twelve miles to Crested Butte, and preached in the evening in the dining-room of the hotel to some forty men and a few women, comprising nearly all who were not away in the mines. Some Congregationalists from Lyons, Iowa, are putting up a smelter here. The country is beautiful, with plenty of grass along the valleys, which are hemmed in by the mountains on every side. Here is a vein of coal forty-two inches thick, which is an important consideration in an isolated camp like this.

The next day, I passed on ten miles to Gothic City, which has an elevation of some nine thousand feet. Here is quite a village.

I preached to a small audience, the men being mostly absent in the mines. I went within a few miles of Gunnison City, the county seat of Gunnison County, which has six or eight families, and is smaller than the towns I visited. Very few persons will remain in the country during the winter. Many are about leaving. Crested Butte and Gothic are in the Elk Mountains, only a few miles from the line of the Ute Reservation, which shuts us out from the region west. Should the mines open favorably, there will be a large immigration in the spring, when a missionary should be put in here, making his head-quarters at Crested Butte, and supplying the camps for twenty miles around.

Returning, I preached at Hillerton, in the post-office building on Broadway. It was the first religious service held in the town. We sang "Coronation." A weekly newspaper published there, *The Occident*, gave an abstract of the services. The weather was very cold, and I suffered severely. Water froze quite thick in a close tent.

At Cottonwood Springs, I found letters from Leadville, informing me of new perplexities and embarrassments in the work there. It was a heavy blow to me. I came down to Cañon City, and home.

Colorado Springs, September 9.—I had hoped for a rest, after the exhausting labors of the past few months, but have to return to Leadville the moment I am through with my correspondence. Have had a delightful visit from a former parishioner at Wentworth (Hon. J. E. Sargent, of Concord, N.H.). How many sweet and hallowed memories it recalls! I have lived again in the past. We have been with him to the Garden of the Gods, Ute Pass, and Glen Eyrie.

I want time to consider what should be done for New Mexico and Utah. The Lord may give our churches a desire to go in and possess them, and may raise up some instrumentality for sending teachers into them, to be followed by missionary labor. I have been absorbed in special localities, so that I have had little opportunity to take a comprehensive view of my field. Yet I

have done what seemed best. I think I have no selfish ambition in these things. The shortness of life, the vanity of human ambition, the littleness of man, have been impressed upon me as never before. Amid the mighty scenes of nature, the Bible has been my constant companion. Its truths have been more to me than the mountain streams.

Leadville, September 16.— I came by the new road by Musquito Pass; but, in going over the wildest and most romantic places, we were in pitchy darkness. There were a large number of women with families coming to meet their husbands, which is cheering to those who want to see moral principles established in the mountains.

The work here must now be looked to. I spent all yesterday going round with the chairman of the building committee. We were fortunate in getting part of the native lumber at twenty dollars, instead of twenty-five. One of the shingle-mills made an offer that the shingle-mills in town should give the shingles. Another seconded the motion. The Lord seems favoring us in our extremity.

September 18.— I collected over one hundred dollars yesterday. I have prayed for hopefulness and cheerfulness in this work of collecting, and especially in meeting with rebuffs that are so discouraging; and I think God is answering my prayer. I fear I did not do just right in going home from Cottonwood Springs, instead of coming back here. I promised God this morning that I would try to be more considerate.

September 22.— The weather is delightful, though the dust in the roads is fearful. I could make up quite a story of the delights of spring. Strawberries are in blossom. The robins are abundant on Capitol Hill, where I walk each morning. A red squirrel cuts up his pranks on the pine-trees near by, seemingly ridiculing my devotions.

Jenks' Station, Dakota, October 1.— The eve is beautiful. The Black Hills show themselves in the west, no longer the gloomy

solitudes I once saw, but brightened by prayer and Christian work, the home of our dear churches.   How the love of God and man changes the face of nature !

October 3.—I left the coach at four o'clock yesterday morning, and took "across lots" to Rockerville, nine miles for breakfast. The morning was wonderfully beautiful, the sky clear as crystal. I called all around, and preached last eve to a large congregation. The church has bought the school-house.   I am to pay twenty-five dollars, and expect to get the money from some source.   This morning after early breakfast I took a walk to Rapid.   When I got where the road led down into a wild ravine, I had to strike across again; but I did better than ever before.   I found a place where the bee line was not perpendicular, and reached Rapid at noon.   The crops have been fine here, without any irrigation, which settles the matter of agriculture.

Deadwood, October 6.—The coach was behind, Saturday.   There were twenty-three passengers, but I was favored in riding with the driver most of the way.   We had over a ton of freight, and came slowly.   Before the moon rose, it was so dark that, with the dust, the smoke of the mountain fires, and piles of baggage, the driver was in continual fear of upsetting us.   But we soon learn to take things as they come.   The fires were grand in the hills, whole hill-sides livid with flame.   We reached here between twelve and one, Sabbath morning.   The moon shone upon the blackened city.   Our parsonage is safe, also the church, which has cost nearly two thousand dollars.   Energy and enterprise are throwing up buildings on every side.   The church is going forward in Central, just in the place where I wanted it.   At Lead, the church is not plastered, but looked nicely, and was dedicated. We had an excellent meeting of the Black Hills Association, organized an Education society, pushed forward plans for the academy at Spearfish, and had an ordination by a council at Central.

Rapid City, October 20.—Starting from Deadwood on Tuesday, I came the next day forty miles, to Custer, the oldest camp in the

Hills, a beautiful location. The old, deserted houses are occupied again. Three years ago there were some thousands of people there, now about two hundred. We got in just as pitchy darkness was gathering around us. A heavy rain came on, the first rain in the Hills for several months. As we left Custer, the wind was terrible on the high table-land. The grass had been burned; and the cinders flew in our faces, with small stones, so that we could not open our eyes. We were obliged to run our horses for several miles. We came here on Friday, and the next day drove up and down this beautiful valley. The camps west of here have taken a new lease of life. Remarkable gold discoveries, recently made, may change the centre of population in the Hills. My trip has been very pleasant and profitable. It does me much good to see our work going forward.

Leadville, Col., October 27.—Reached here at two P.M., Saturday. It now takes two whole days to come from Denver. I found the church up, and shingled, four men at work. As I looked at it, I lifted up my heart to God and rejoiced. But the church is in debt, and I must help. We want to push the work this beautiful weather, if we can get the money. I have prayed that God may go before us, and open the hearts of this people.

After another week of untiring labor at Leadville, Mr. Pickett returned to Colorado Springs. He marked the first Sunday of November as a "sweet day of rest" with his family, and in the afternoon read to them Longfellow's "Children of the Lord's Supper." Rev. Harlan P. Roberts, of Silverton, who had been a member of his household at Mount Pleasant, was with them. A few days afterward, the Colorado Association met at Colorado Springs. He enjoyed the interchange of cordial greetings with his brethren, as they came together from their widely separated fields, and took part in their discussions with reference to the

7

Indian question, education in New Mexico, Renan's view of Christ, church music, and progress in religion. He reported to them fully his own work, and awakened such interest and sympathy that the consideration of another subject which had been assigned to follow his report was postponed; and the Association gave itself to prayer for the fields in which he had labored and for the success of home missions in the regions beyond. The officers of the American Home Missionary Society at New York had requested him at the earliest possible moment to visit Utah, and open up several incipient preaching stations. This he was intent to do, and was only waiting, in order to complete the church at Leadville, so that it could be occupied for services of public worship. Saturday, he joined his brethren in a pleasure excursion to Cheyenne cañon, and on the Sabbath taught his wife's Bible-class of young ladies, shared in the joy of the dedication of a house of worship erected by the Congregational Church at Colorado Springs, and took part in a missionary meeting in the evening, at which a liberal offering was made for the church at Leadville.

Tuesday, after a season of "precious devotion," as he entered in his diary, and words of love and counsel to dear ones, and an affectionate note to his mother, who had sent him some mittens of her own make for his comfort in the approaching winter, he was, as he wrote to her, "off in a few minutes for Leadville." With friends on the train, he indulged in a cheerful vein of humor, as was natural to him in social inter-

course. The two following days he spent in Denver, soliciting help for the church at Leadville, and writing nineteen letters to as many mine-owners at the East for the same object. He also purchased windows and seats for the church, and was planning to have it ready for occupancy on the second Sabbath following. "We cannot wait till spring," he said. "Spring comes too late upon the mountains. I must hurry, and keep the workmen at that church." In a letter to Mrs. Pickett, he sent his love to the boys, and said, "Tell them I am going to ask, when I come, which of them did the most to make our home the happiest, brightest spot on earth." He led a church prayer-meeting Wednesday evening, and the following day had an interview with the Governor of Colorado, who gave him good reports of the work at Silverton, and of the missionary there, and also encouraged him with sympathy and aid for the church at Leadville. He heard favorable opinions expressed as to his own labors, and was assured of the growing regard and esteem that was felt for himself and for his work throughout the mountain region. Mentioning this, in writing to his wife, he added, "May we give reputation, influence, life itself, to Him who gave so much for us!" This was on the 13th of November. That evening, he took the train on the Denver, South Park, and Pacific Railroad, in a snow-storm, and the following morning sent his usual message as to where he was, and of affection to his family, with the words: "On cars, South Park, midst of snow-storm. Hope to get over range without trouble."

The storm was of extreme violence; the winds blew a tempest; the snow was a foot deep, and obstructed the headway of the train. The end of the track, which was then at Weston, one hundred and eight miles from Denver, was not reached until four hours after the schedule time. The storm was then at its height. Some of the passengers were inclined to lie over until the next day. But hoping to get over the worst of the road before sunset, and intent on reaching their home or their business at Leadville, and having a careful and reliable driver, who had driven through many a mountain storm, it was decided to go on. Mr. Pickett was well acquainted with the driver, having rode with him several times on former journeys, and on this occasion requested him to reserve the seat which he occupied. There were fourteen passengers, nine inside the coach, three of whom were ladies, and five on the outside. Mr. Pickett was among the latter, his seat by the driver. They started shortly after noon, Friday, November 14th, with buffalo robes, wraps, and blankets to protect them from the cold. It was a rough drive to Platte Station, the snow blowing in such clouds that it was impossible to see any length ahead. Even the horses at times could not be seen. At this place, the driver told the passengers that they might remain over night, if they preferred. Still hoping, however, to get over the worst of the road at least, before night, they said that they would proceed, if the driver was willing. He expressed no hesitation, and the battle with the storm was resumed.

The first delay was in ascending Weston Pass, caused by a freighter's wagon, which blocked the road, until a team from a wagon in front came to its assistance. Nearly half an hour was lost at this point. The snow and hail continued to come down furiously, almost blinding those on the outside. Once or twice, they became so chilled that they alighted, and walked a short distance to warm themselves. On one of these occasions, Mr. Pickett remarked that he did not like being locked up in the boot, because it would be difficult to escape in case of an accident. He further stated that he had tried, but was not able to unbuckle the straps. He expressed his confidence in the driver, and said that he thought no accident would occur while he held the reins. Shortly after, he resumed his seat in the boot, and was in good spirits.

Another delay was occasioned by freighters, who were stalled on a hill near Lower Rocky Station. An hour passed before this obstruction was removed. It was now nearly dark. From this place, the coach went along smoothly, until about seven o'clock, when the driver stopped his six horses, and warmed his hands by slapping them across his body, to get the right feeling in them, as he said, for the extra exertion required in going down the mountain. Then they rushed along at rapid gait. The sleet and snow were blowing in blinding fury, freezing to the face. In descending a steep pitch on sideling ground, about eleven miles from Leadville, the driver put on the brake; but it became obstructed with snow, and would

not hold. He made a desperate effort to pull in the horses; but they became unmanageable, and sheered to the left, to avoid the brunt of the storm. Here the coach upset, turning completely over on its top. The outside passengers were thrown away from or under it; and those inside were thrown on their heads, with their feet up. The horses became uncoupled, and pulled over the driver, who was holding the reins firmly. He escaped with a severe injury on his shoulder. The injured passengers slowly and painfully extricated themselves from the wreck. In the confusion, the bruised and wounded received attention first. No person in the company had a match to strike a light or kindle a fire. Nearly an hour elapsed before it was found that Mr. Pickett was fastened in by the boot-apron, and was dead. As the coach went over, he was heard to exclaim, "O my God!" He was killed instantly. His neck was broken. To appropriate to him language in which, a short time previously, he had depicted the moment after death, — "Time was no more. The struggles and weariness of earth were ended. The responsibilities of life were laid down. The Rocky Mountains and the great globe faded away. The white hills of Paradise dawned, bathed in everlasting righteousness; and he saw the city which hath foundations, and the King in his beauty."

As soon as his remains were taken from the wreck, three of the passengers walked to the Nine-mile House for assistance; and the next day the body was removed to Leadville. A meeting of the Protestant pastors of

the city was convened in the evening at the Methodist parsonage, and resolutions of respect for his memory as "a good man and an earnest and eloquent preacher of Christ, who had fallen at his post, and had gone to receive a crown of righteousness," were adopted; and arrangements were made for funeral services to be held at the Presbyterian church Sunday afternoon. The pastors acted· as pall-bearers. Though the weather was cold and snow was falling, the house was filled to overflowing; and the whole community attested their sympathy and their regard for one who had laid down his life in the service of Christ and his fellow-men. Impressive addresses were delivered by Rev. R. Weiser and Rev. Charles R. Bliss.

At Colorado Springs, the news of the calamity broke with fearful shock upon his family and friends. The body was brought to the desolated home November 19. On the following day, appropriate services were held at the Congregational church. Many came from near and far, testifying the love and respect in which Mr. Pickett was cherished. The pastor, Rev. R. T. Cross, gave an address, reviewing his life and labors and portraying his character, from which the following extracts are taken : —

We are all mourners to-day. Our souls are bowed down with a great grief, our hearts are crushed with a great sorrow. Like little children, we stand in the presence of this strange scene, wondering what it means. Yet not for one moment do we doubt God's overruling providence, nor distrust his wisdom, goodness, and love. For, if we give up our faith in these, all is gone; and we stand no longer on a solid rock. Bowing then in grief, but

without a murmur, to the will of God, let us look at our brother's life. . . .

His was a successful life, a grand and glorious life, because it was a Christ-like life.

1. In his genial, affable, friendly spirit toward every one whom he met. Those who only casually met him noticed it. When entering upon his superintendency in Iowa, he laid down certain principles or rules that he strove to follow. The first one was, " I shall try to avoid that cold, indifferent manner, characteristic of agents and others who travel and mingle much with men. I shall pray for a warm, Christ-like heart, glowing with love and sympathy for *all*. I shall endeavor even among crowds of strangers to feel that Christ died for them, and shall pray that they may be delivered from sin, and become his followers." Many can witness to the faithful manner in which he carried out this resolve.

2. Indomitable energy, great enthusiasm and hopefulness, burning zeal, and a spirit of self-sacrifice were prominent elements of his character. The way in which he pushed the work in the Black Hills, and the way in which he was pushing the work of building a church at Leadville, were proofs of his energy. Where others saw great obstacles he saw them too; but he saw also a mightier power, and was hopeful and enthusiastic in regard to the hardest fields. The burning zeal for upbuilding the Redeemer's kingdom, for which he prayed when a student, was his to the end. Nothing could quench it. It burned brighter and brighter to the last. " I will pray," he said, " that this lovely Iowa may be given to the Saviour for his inheritance." And that was his prayer for Colorado and the new West. On the fly-leaf of Fossett's *Colorado*, which he presented to his wife on her birthday, he wrote: " Shall it not be our daily prayer, my dear wife, that as I have given you this book, and written your name upon it, so Christ may give us this State, that we, when life's work is done, may give it to him with his own name written in enduring characters on all its mountains and valleys and precious things?"

In addition to his self-sacrifice for the churches, let me speak of another and costlier sacrifice. For nearly ten years, he was a

widower, with no home. When he established a home here, he enjoyed it intensely. It was a quiet haven for him, a little heaven on earth, when he returned from his tedious journeys. Yet for months he was away from that home, spending the time in rough mining-camps, with few comforts, and no conveniences for study. At one time, he was absent nearly four months; and, of the eighteen months he has been in Colorado, he spent only about four at home. This costly sacrifice he made for the Master's sake.

3. He was a man of prayer. He walked with God continually. He prayed daily for the Home Missionary Society, and for all the churches and pastors on his field. As soon as we heard him talk and pray when he came to Colorado, we knew that he was the right man; and we thanked God for sending him. Although pastor of the church to which he belonged, I looked upon him as our pastor, and shall feel his loss most keenly. His prayers had much to do, I have no doubt, with the blessings which this church has received. In lonely forests, on mountain-tops, and in dark cañons, he pleaded with God. Often he would take his Bible and go up on the mountain-side, and, looking down, as Christ did upon Jerusalem,. plead for the mining-camp at his feet. His memory will have no nobler monument than his work in the Black Hills: seven churches, five ministers on the ground, four church buildings, three parsonages, an association, a Bible society, and an academy,—all the work of about one year. But the key to that wonderful work is found, as he has told us, in that day when, detained by high water at Jenney's Stockade, he took his Bible, went out into the fields, and spent the day in prayer for the Black Hills. As he prayed, the whole work opened before him, just as it was afterwards carried out.

Words cannot express the sympathy we feel for the afflicted family and friends. We can only point them to the promises, to the joyful hope and triumphant faith of that gospel which their loved one preached so faithfully. And what a glorious legacy he has left you! If all the mines of the Rocky Mountains were owned by one man, and he should die and leave them to his family, he would not leave so rich, so precious, so grand a legacy

as your loved one has left you,—the legacy of a spotless name, a noble Christian life.

Fellow-laborers in Christ's vineyard, ministers and laymen of every denomination, as we stand by the lifeless form of this faithful servant of God, let us consecrate ourselves anew to the work for which he laid down his life. He gave his life for the church at Leadville, but in a larger sense he gave it for the whole church of Christ on earth. He was a chosen and trusted leader in one division of the church militant, but he fought under the banner of our common Christianity. Let us follow in his footsteps, because they were the footsteps of the Master.

Beloved brother, your life has not been in vain. The world is better for your having lived in it. Your example is an inspiration to us all. You have kept the faith, and now you have received the crown of rejoicing from the Lord.

As the report of his sudden death was borne over the land, many hearts were stricken as with a personal bereavement. The miners and ranchmen of the Rocky Mountains joined in lamentation with the dwellers upon the prairies.

> "The beauty of Israel is slain upon thy high places:
> How are the mighty fallen in the midst of the battle!"

At Denver, one said, "Nothing since Lincoln's death has given us such a shock and such sinking of heart." The Black Hills were filled with sadness. Memorial services were held at Lead City and Deadwood, also at Mount Pleasant, Iowa. Former scholars and parishioners, and his brethren in the ministry, recorded their remembrances of his sympathetic and generous nature, his fine Christian enthusiasm, his fervid devotion, and his unselfish life:—

He was a soldier; but his kindly, congenial nature won over

men instead of arousing their hostility. He was so inconsiderate of self, so full of abiding trust in his Master, that even the strongest natures could not withhold their respect. What struck me on first acquaintance was his abounding hopefulness and cheerfulness, never yielding to despondency or discouragement, but finding comfort and strength where others saw only clouds and darkness. His special and continued regard for the church at Mount Pleasant was manifested in so many ways as to demand mention and the life-long respect of all who find in it a spiritual home. Up to the removal of his children, in 1877, he was a regular contributor to the maintenance of its services, paying from fifty to one hundred dollars annually out of his meagre salary as missionary superintendent. JOHN TEESDALE.

One who knew him both in Iowa and in the Black Hills wrote:—

It has been my pleasure to know Mr. Pickett intimately from near the beginning of his pastorate at Mount Pleasant. I remember how active he then was in the duties pertaining to his charge, how he worked for the young people, visited the schools, taking more interest than any of the other pastors, and was zealous in every good work. Afterwards, he entered a wider field, and became a missionary through Southern Iowa, carrying to weak points words of courage, and to suffering hearts consolation and hope. His efficiency and zeal as a Christian apostle induced the Missionary Society to send him to Colorado and Western Dakota, where he labored among the rude spirits of the frontier, the unorganized elements of the mining-camps. Church after church sprung up as the result of his toil, and hundreds of people were led by his teaching to a better life. He had such kind, earnest, sincere ways, without ostentation, without hypocrisy. Rough men would suppress an oath and sacrilegious jest, when he was near. Scoffers at religion would go to hear him preach, when they would hear no other. At the homes and firesides of the frontier, he had a cheering word, a sunny smile, to lighten the burdens and brighten

the pathway of life. We shall hear no more his cordial greeting, shake no more his friendly hand, nor hear his earnest words, warning men not to do evil, exhorting them to do good. Yet he still lives in the memory of his earnest labor and bright example. In the hearts of the people, he built his monument. All who knew him praise the Great Giver for the lesson of his noble life.

EDWIN VAN CISE.

Mr. Pickett impressed me with a marvellous religious energy and enthusiasm. It was the zeal of the Lord of hosts. Stanch in his faith, he was no bigot. There was room in his heart and welcome for all who loved the cross, whatever other divergences there might be. A Church of Christ without other name than that of the Master would have been his preference. I never met a man more sanguine in his spirit, less inclined to count odds in questions of the Kingdom and its advancement. I shall not forget the conqueror spirit with which at Leadville he claimed for Jesus the ground on which Satan was intrenched.

CHARLES C. SALTER,
Pastor at Denver, 1877–79.

To us, no man in Colorado seemed more needed, and no man in our ministerial ranks appeared more fitted for the peculiar and important work he was called to do. A prince indeed has fallen in Israel. No one who heard him and observed his movements at the Association could doubt his readiness for the translation. We could not fail to see that he had been with Jesus. The Master was seen in his burning zeal and earnest prayers, in his thoughts that breathed a deeper spiritual life, in his passion for souls, in his sweetness of spirit, and in his extreme watchfulness and jealousy lest anything should hinder the Kingdom. His life motto, carried into practice, seemed to be, "All and always for Christ."

JOSEPH ADAMS,
Cottonwood Springs, Colorado.

He was well fitted for his work. It was hard; but he loved it. His whole soul was in it. He understood men, and knew how to take hold of them. He never needed a second introduction. He was a man of noble courage. He smiled at self-denial. So, too, he was a most thoughtful and considerate man. The drivers of the stage-coaches upon which he travelled knew him. He could call them by name, and tell you much of their history. These drivers have lost a friend. C. M. SANDERS,

Pastor at Cheyenne, Wyoming Territory.

He brought to Colorado from his superintendency in Iowa an amount of experience, sagacity, enthusiasm, energy, and personal attractions that specially fitted him for his post amid the peculiar conditions and social elements of the mountains. A more truly spiritual, devout, consecrated man we have rarely met. "Always about his Father's business," could be said as truly of few men. We can hardly think of that tireless spirit as at rest. With his whole soul intent on his work, at a time when it would seem he could ill be spared, the Master's word summoned him to other activities in a higher sphere. There was but an instant's notice; yet who can doubt the prompt response of that ever-girded soul, "Here am I"? His memory will long be cherished as his work will be felt.

The Home Missionary, 1880.

LINES SUGGESTED BY THE DEATH OF REV. JOSEPH W. PICKETT.

"He is dead among the mountains!"
Thus the ringing message sped;
And a thousand hearts' deep fountains
Stirred with grief, and tears were shed;
And the East land and the West land
Felt a loss beyond repair,
When they heard the dreadful message,
When they knew the dead was there.

Ne'er did Colorado's mountains,
  Since they reared their rock-ribbed sides
From the plain that once encased them
  Into "continent divides,"
Echo back so sad a story,
  So supremely sad, I trow,
As this fearful death in darkness,
  'Mid the blinding sleet and snow.

Ah, how hard it was to drink it !—
  This, the dregs of sorrow's cup.
Ah, how long we could not think it,—
  Could not, would not, give him up !
How we reasoned that the missive
  Had most surely been misread !
But the lightning-voice repeated,
  "He is in the mountains, dead."

Dead ! yes, dead ! No more we'll meet him,
  Hear no more his ringing voice.
Home and friends no more will greet him,
  In his love no more rejoice.
Overwhelmed with grief and sorrow,
  Sad they wait, but wait in vain :
He who left so late, so brightly,
  Ne'er can light that home again.

But, amid its gloom and sadness,
  Comes sweet consolation's breath,
Bringing whispered words of gladness,
  Gilding e'en the cloud of death ;
Telling that, with strength unbated,
  From the battle's thickest strife,
Like the saint of old, translated,
  He was ushered into life.

Toil and strife for him thus ending,
  Every duty nobly done,
Leaving memories full of blessing,
  Loved and mourned by every one,

In a moment, in a twinkling,
From earth's mountains, cold and bare,
Passed he to the hills eternal,
Everlasting joys to share.

From the darkness and the tempest,
And the chilling, freezing blasts,
To the light and warmth of Beulah,
Where the spring-time ever lasts,—
Thus he passed ; but left his mantle,
E'en a life so noble, pure,
That its fragrance will continue
Long as love and truth endure.

I knew him intimately since 1856. Was with him the two years he taught in Tennessee. The record of his life should be kept as an inspiration to every struggling soul.

J. W. PHILLIPS.

St. Louis, November, 1879.

Mr. Pickett was of a sanguine-nervous temperament. With Christian zeal aflame, and with great openings for usefulness before him, it was his nature to overwork. His ardor and activity would carry him beyond bounds ; but, though exhausted with excessive labors, and sometimes losing patience with those who had less persistence and endurance, and speaking unadvisedly, he was rarely depressed, and was without moroseness or mixture of melancholy. His spiritual energy seemed to rebound from every fatigue. He exercised careful scrutiny over himself, and ruled and restrained his spirit with strict discipline. The grace and virtue he attained came not without painstaking and prayer. A deep consciousness of sin and humility of mind were among the foundations of his religious life.

Thoroughly independent and self-reliant, his nature was equally genial and fraternal. He made others' joys and sorrows his own. No one prized Christian fellowship more, or would go farther to maintain it.

With his brethren in the ministry and with the executive officers of the American Home Missionary Society, he was in cordial relations. Warm in his domestic attachments, he was scrupulous as to any encroachment upon his missionary work. The only temporal provision that he made was in carrying a small life-insurance policy. He gave unusual consideration to the words of Christ about leaving all for his sake and the gospel's. But he would not allow one duty to dispense with another. In absences from home, daily epistles to his family bore to them his love and care.

With frequent opportunities before him for profitable business ventures and for investments in lands and in mines, he never turned aside to any of them, but kept himself wholly intent upon his work. He followed closely the sentiment of the apostle, which he made his daily motto for years : —

This one thing I do, forgetting those things which are behind, and reaching forth unto those things which are before, I press toward the mark for the prize of the high calling of God in Christ Jesus.— *Phil.* iii., 13, 14.

On one occasion, in the Black Hills, going over from Lead City to Central, he discovered some fine specimens of ore, and gathered them up in his handkerchief. But finding himself pondering upon them and their

probable value, and upon making a mining-claim, and perceiving that the matter was taking some hold ·of his mind, and that it might distract his thoughts, he at once shook his handkerchief to the winds, and, repeating aloud his motto, knelt upon the ground, and renewed his consecration to his life-work.

The evangelization of our country, the establishment of churches and institutions of Christian education in the new States, was the passion of his life. In this work, he was ready to hold fellowship with all true believers ; and he encouraged their union in one Christian church, wherever it was practicable in new communities, and in those of limited population. In harmony with these sentiments, he prosecuted his missionary labors, and planted churches in the interior of the continent, and in vast mountain regions. In Iowa, he introduced moral and religious order in numerous places, carried saving health into thousands of homes, and gave powerful support to churches, schools, and colleges. To the Rocky Mountains, he brought greater treasures than their mines will ever yield. Visiting from house to house, from cabin to cabin, and from mine to mine, and preaching with a prophet's fervor, he organized Christian society, and laid foundations for the development of the kingdom of God in righteousness and peace.

> " How beautiful upon the mountains
> Are the feet of him that bringeth good tidings,
> That publisheth peace,
> That bringeth good tidings of good,
> That publisheth salvation,
> That saith unto Zion, Thy God reigneth ! "

He rests from his labors, and his works do follow him. Others have entered into them. The church at Leadville recovered from the shock occasioned by his death, and completed and dedicated their house of worship on the first Sabbath in June, 1880. They gave it the name of the Pickett Memorial Church, and placed his portrait upon the wall. The Spearfish Academy is rising into usefulness and honor. The corner-stone of a new building for its use was laid by the governor of Dakota Territory, July 24, 1880.

It remains for many brave and valiant men to carry forward these labors, and plant the gospel over all these regions, and possess the New West and the continent in the name of the Lord Jesus, with Christian homes and schools and churches. This volume has been prepared in the fond hope that its record of earnest devotion to the work may awaken a similar spirit of consecration in some generous bosoms, and also call forth liberal offerings of silver and gold for the support of home missions and Christian education in the United States.

William Salter

Memoirs of Joseph W. Pickett

missionary superintendent in southern Iowa and in the Rocky mountains for the

American home missionary society